W9-CLS-209

The Bilbao
Looking Glass

The Bilbao Looking Glass

CHARLOTTE MACLEOD

Thorndike Press • Thorndike, Maine

THE JEFFERSON-MADISON
REGIONAL LIBRARY
CHARLOTTESVILLE, VA.

LP
m
MacLeod
Cop 1

Library of Congress Cataloging in Publication Data:

MacLeod, Charlotte.
  The Bilbao looking glass.

1. Large type books.   I. Title
[PS3563.A31865B5   1983b]   813'.54   83-9100
ISBN 0-89621-467-2 (lg. print)

Copyright 1983 by Charlotte MacLeod. All the characters in
this book are fictitious, and any resemblance to actual persons,
living or dead, is purely coincidental.

From "Mending Wall" from *The Poetry of Robert Frost* edited
by Edward Connery Lathem. Copyright 1930, 1939, © 1969
by Holt, Rinehart & Winston. Copyright © 1958 by Robert
Frost. Copyright © 1967 by Lesley Frost. Ballantine. Reprinted
by permission of Holt, Rinehart & Winston Publishers.

Large Print edition available through arrangement with
Doubleday & Company, Inc., New York.

Cover design by Armen Kojoyian.

For Peggy Barrett

CHAPTER 1

"Where on earth," said Sarah Kelling of the Boston Kellings "did that looking glass come from?"

"Spain."

Max Bittersohn eased a basketful of Sarah's personal effects to the floor. This was the first time he'd ever been in the front entryway of the clapboard ark known to the Kelling family since Grover Cleveland's day as the Ireson's Landing place.

"Actually," he amended, "nobody's ever found out for sure where those marble-framed looking glasses were made. Seamen during the eighteenth century used to pick them up at the port of Bilbao and bring them home to their wives and sweethearts. That was before scrimshawed corset busks came into vogue, I believe. Whatever possessed you to leave a valuable thing like that hanging in your summer house all winter?"

"But I didn't. That's just the point. It doesn't belong here. I've never seen the glass before."

"I'll be damned." Bittersohn leaned forward and inspected the handsome little antique with the eye of an expert, which in fact he was. "Mind if I take this off the wall?"

"Why should I? I've just told you it's not mine."

"And I believe you, heart of my heart, because you'd have rocks in your head not to claim a Bilbao looking glass if you had any excuse to. Furthermore, I deduce from the marks on this revolting wallpaper that some larger object has been hanging here until recently. What was that?"

"A swoony old mezzotint called 'Love's Awakening.' I took it back to Tulip Street last winter to decorate Cousin Theonia's room."

"And look what you started."

Bittersohn spoke absentmindedly. He'd taken out a pocket magnifying glass and was examining the graceful pinky-yellow marble pilasters of the delicate frame in approved Sherlockian manner. "I wish there were more light in this vestibule, or whatever the hell you call it."

"Your wish is my command," Sarah flipped a wall switch. "Or would have been," she amended when nothing happened, "if I'd remembered to tell Mr. Lomax to turn on the electricity. He'll be along pretty soon, I expect. I told him this was official moving day."

"Did you tell him I'd be moving in, too?"

"I expect so. Anyway, he knew I was fixing up the apartment for a tenant because he did most of the work, and he must have realized somebody would be driving me since I don't have a car of my own now."

"I said I'd be glad to give you one for a wedding present."

Bittersohn diverted his attention from their interesting find long enough to convince Sarah that his offer still held. "If you'd quit changing your mind from one day to the next — "

"Max, I am not changing my mind. I need time to get squared away, that's all. You needn't resort to bribery and corruption."

"What would it take to corrupt you?" His free hand roved up inside her jersey.

"Stop that, you sex maniac. I thought

9

you were going to deduce how that looking glass got into this house."

"What looking glass?"

"Max, you're not being fair."

"I could be fairer, wert thou less fair. How's that for a courtly turn of phrase?"

Nevertheless, Bittersohn managed to wrest his attention back to the charming artifact that had so unexpectedly usurped the place of "Love's Awakening."

"Got a towel or something?"

"I'll look in the kitchen. Would you settle for a couple of pot holders?"

"Anything. It's just to protect the frame in case of fingerprints."

"Max darling, do you really do things like that?"

"I might if you'd get me those pot holders."

"Oh, sorry."

Sarah went away and came back in a minute or so with a length of mildewed curtain.

"Will this do? It's all I could find."

"Admirably. Hold the front door open, will you? I want to carry the looking glass out into the light where I can get a decent look at it, and I don't want to bash the top on the way."

"That little gesso urn and the gilded wire ornamentation do look awfully fragile."

"They are. That's why you find so few Bilbao looking glasses in mint condition, which I shouldn't be surprised if this turned out to be."

Bittersohn wrapped the musty-smelling curtain around the frame and lifted gently. "Damn, it's stuck. See what that wire's caught on, will you? Don't touch the frame if you can help it."

"It's all right to touch the wire, I suppose?"

"Oh sure. Picture wire wouldn't take a print."

"Wait a second, it's twisted around the hook. There, now lift. The wire looks brand new, Max."

"That doesn't surprise me. Whoever owns this thing probably kept it screwed to the wall. See those little flanges at the sides? All looking glasses used to have them back at that time. Mirrors were too scarce and valuable to take chances with."

"I know. They even used to build a solid wood panel into the parlor wall to fasten the mirror into because plaster was too insecure. Aunt Appie has one at her house in Cambridge."

"She's the aunt whose husband just died?"

"Yes, Uncle Samuel had been ailing for years, from one thing and another. Cousin Mabel always said what really ailed him was Aunt Appie, but what else could one expect from Cousin Mabel? Are those wormholes in the backing?"

"Si, señora. That's a hunk of oak paneling, which is characteristically Spanish and heavy as hell. These holes were undoubtedly chewed by genuine eighteenth-century Spanish oakworms. You could always tell them because they had a habit of shouting 'Olé' before they sunk in their little fangs. Some people will try to tell you Bilbao looking glasses were really made in Italy, which is nonsense. Italian oakworms couldn't have done this much damage. They'd only say, *Poco poco, lente lente,* which is Italian for 'The hell with it, let's send out for a pizza.' "

"Spare me your erudition," Sarah sniffed. "Max, I don't honestly give a hoot where this looking glass originally came from. I just want to know who parked it in my front entryway."

"You don't suppose one of your rich relatives snuck in and hung it here as a nice little housewarming surprise, do you?"

"Huh! Show me a Kelling who'd leave a

valuable antique unguarded in a place like this, and I'll show you six other Kellings trying to get him certified as a raving lunatic."

"Well, can you think of one who owns a Bilbao looking glass?"

"One of them must, I suppose, considering how many relatives I have and how much junk they've amassed over the years. I believe Aunt Emma out in Longmeadow has something like this, come to think of it, but the marble's more yellowish and the top has a hideous walnut pediment instead of this pretty filigree."

"I'm not surprised. That's what generally happened. The tops would get broken and the owners would stick on any abomination that happened to be kicking around the woodshed. Even bastardized like that, a genuine Bilbao looking glass will sell for five thousand dollars and up. You know what, *süssele?* I think we ought to call the cops."

"Oh, Max!"

But he was right, of course. This precious oblong of fragility hadn't got into the house by itself, and nobody was supposed to have a key except Sarah and Lomax, the caretaker. There had been robberies again this winter around the mostly shut-up summer colony, as there had been for the past several years. No burglar would have wasted his time trying to steal anything from the Kelling house, but he could have found this isolated estate a handy parking-place for his loot. That meant he'd be coming back for the looking glass.

"All right," she sighed. "Do you suppose we might ask for that darling Sergeant Jofferty?"

It had been Sergeant Jofferty who'd come to tell her about the crash, here to this very drive from which she'd waved good-bye to Alexander. He'd looked so happy then, setting out with his blind mother for what he didn't know would be his last drive in the 1920 Milburn Electric that had been his greatest love, after Sarah herself. Last November, that had been. It was early June now, almost seven months later. One might think she'd have got over the pain, but it kept coming back at odd moments. That was why she still couldn't do what Max Bittersohn wanted; what she herself wanted except at times like this when she started thinking about the elderly, handsome, tortured husband she'd loved so long and lost so shatteringly.

"I know Jofferty," Max replied a shade

14

unds. Sarah would have preferred the
oths and the Vandals. She could only steer
em to where the poison ivy grew thickest,
d pray for lots of mosquitos.

They'd have to stay clear of the garden
nyway. This year, Sarah and Mr. Lomax
ere going in for gardening on the grand
cale. The old caretaker's nephew Pete, who
vas allegedly helping him, had borrowed a
.... from some crony or other and
.... that, he

too quickly. He knew what was in her
mind. He always did, somehow. "Is the
phone working?"

"It ought to be. I wrote them to resume
service as of the first of June. The number
for the police is on that pad."

In Alexander's small, meticulous hand-
writing. Sometime soon she'd have to go
through the house and remove all those
stabbing little reminders. It would be like
killing him all over again. When Max
looked up from dialing, he saw that Sarah
was crying. He gave her a twisted smile,
half compassion, half exasperation, and
pulled her close to him while he talked.

"Is Sergeant Jofferty around? Then could
you get him on the car radio? Tell him
Mrs. Kelling out at Ireson's Landing has
something to show him. No, thank God,
nothing like that. It's just something that
made her wonder if someone's been trying
to break in. Oh, sure, I'm her tenant, Max
Bittersohn. Ira Rivkin's brother-in-law.
Right, I'll tell Ira you said so."

He hung up and fished out his handkerchief. "Here, blow your nose. I hope you
understand I'm only trying to keep you
from getting into another mess."

"I know, Max. It isn't that." She sniffled

and blew. "It's — you know perfectly well what it is. Why don't you go get the rest of my stuff out of your car while I take this basket up and start unpacking? What shall we do with the looking glass?"

"Hang it back where we found it till Jofferty gets here. Don't worry, Sarah."

Still holding the frame through the scrap of old curtain, Bittersohn put the mirror on its hook, then went out to get Sarah's suitcases while she lugged the basket to her second floor bedroom.

A few weeks ago, on her twenty-seventh birthday, she'd taken control of a trust fund her father had left her, and dipped gingerly into the capital to replace some of the furnishings she'd looted from Ireson's Landing last winter when she'd turned her Beacon Hill brownstone into a boarding house. There was a new mattress in her room and another in the carriage house for Max. He was to have what used to be the coachman's quarters. The relatives would have thought it too scandalous for him to sleep at the main house until such time as he and Sarah were well and duly linked in matrimony. More important, having the carriage house operable would give them both a place to hide out when the estate got too thickly

overrun with self-invited Kellings, as it a suredly would be at various times durin the summer.

Max could flee to his own relatives things got too desperate. He had parent not far away in Saugus and a married siste living among the year-rounders over at the other side of Ireson Town. Sarah had been casually acquainted for ages with Miriam's husband Ira, who owned the local garage and their son Mi local garage, her son Mike, who pumped gas when he wasn't attending classes at Boston University. She'd recently been taken to meet Miriam, too. After a rather stiff first visit with everybody sitting around the living room making polite conversation and being pressed by their hostess to consume a staggering variety of hors d'oeuvres, they'd got down to real talk over tea and muffins around the kitchen table.

The Rivkins' freewheeling hospitality was a welcome contrast to the rigidly structured system into which Sarah had been born and from which, try as she might, she couldn't seem to escape. Aunt Appie was already booked to arrive the following Monday. Her son Lionel had taken it for granted that he and his four sons were included in the invitation. They intended to camp out on the

Rototiller from ~~~~~ ripped up about half an acre. After tha and his uncle had dug in a smelly truckload of fish heads and offal brought in from the docks in Gloucester.

The fish heads were still attracting flocks of sea gulls. Mr. Lomax tried to make Sarah believe this had been part of his overall game plan since the gulls would contribute their droppings, further to enrich the soil. However, he'd had to replant the squash and beans twice, and they'd given up completely on the corn.

Green peas and early lettuce were already helping to feed Sarah's boarders back on Beacon Hill, though, and she took comfort from the circumstance that the most viable campsite for Lionel and his pestilential brood was downwind of the fish heads. She was sharing this happy thought with Max when Sergeant Jofferty drove up in his cruiser.

"Well, Mrs. Kelling. Nice to see you looking so chipper."

The sergeant didn't exactly cock an eyebrow in Max's direction, but Sarah blushed anyway. "You're looking well, too, Sergeant Jofferty. Do you know Max Bittersohn?"

"Ira Rivkin's brother-in-law, right?" He got out of the car and shook Max's hand. "Glad to meet you. Ira talks about you a lot. Claims you're his rich relative, but with the price of gas these days, I guess Ira's raking in a few bucks himself, eh?"

"Unfortunately, he has to hand it all back to the oil companies," snarled Max.

"Let's not get started on the oil companies," Sarah interposed. "We seem to have another little mystery here, Sergeant Jofferty. When we came in about fifteen minutes ago, we found something that doesn't belong. Max is going to be renting my carriage house for the summer," she found it necessary to explain.

"My aunt, who's just been widowed too, will be staying with me. However, that's neither here nor there. The point is, we opened the door and discovered this looking glass hanging on the wall here in the entryway. Max says it's valuable and I have no idea how it got into my house. Mr. Lomax is the only person other than myself who's supposed to have a key, and you know Jed Lomax."

Naturally, Jofferty knew Jed Lomax. Like Sarah, he refused to entertain any notion that the caretaker could have got up to something even the slightest bit shady. While he was getting Max to tell him the probable market value of a genuine Bilbao looking glass in first-rate condition, the old man himself drove up in his fishy-smelling truck. As they'd expected, Lomax didn't know a thing.

"I can't rightly recall ever seein' that glass before, Miz Kelling. Kind o' pretty, if you like them sort o' things. Say, how come you got the front door open, anyways? You folks always go in the side."

"I know, but my handbag's crammed with stuff and this was the first key I could find. Otherwise, the glass might have hung there all summer and I wouldn't have noticed. This is such a poky little entry that it's never used except when somebody comes to the front door who doesn't know any better. But you do check the doors, Mr. Lomax."

"I do, an' I done it yesterday same as always. Never seen no sign o' breakin' an' enterin', or I'd o' reported it. You been around to look, Max?"

"You two know each other?" Jofferty asked in some surprise.

"Hell, yes, that's Isaac Bittersohn's boy from Saugus. Known 'im since he was knee-high to a flounder. Yep, that's the one that busted his mother's heart."

The caretaker shook his grizzled head, the long peak of the filthy swordfisherman's cap he wore summer and winter wagging sadly from side to side.

"Miz Bittersohn, she swore up, down, an' sideways Max was goin' to come one mighty cropper when he started that crazy business of his 'stead o' studyin' to be a rich doctor like she wanted 'im to. Then he went an' made a liar out of 'er. Been a sad disappointment, first an' last."

Lomax would hardly have gone so far as to smile, but he did give Mrs. Bittersohn's sad disappointment a look that might almost have been called amiable. "Joff, if Max here tells you this lookin' glass is worth stealin', then I'll bet you my bottom dollar it's been stole. An' you may lay to that."

CHAPTER 2

Embarrassed at having gone so far as to commit himself to a definite opinion, Lomax shuffled his feet, hitched at his galluses, and adjusted his cap.

"You need me to help settle, Miz Kelling? If not, I better go stake them tomato plants."

"One thing before you go, Jed," said Max. "Forget you ever saw this looking glass, eh?"

"But why?" Sarah protested. "If it belongs in one of the other houses Mr. Lomax takes care of — "

"The owners may begin wondering how it happened to wind up in your house instead of theirs," Max finished for her.

"Oh. But surely they'd never — " Sarah faltered. She'd forgotten for the moment that Mr. Lomax had a helper this year.

From what little she'd seen of that nephew, she wondered if perhaps the Lomax reputation for probity might be in danger of getting tarnished around the edges. Pete would hardly hide stolen property here, though, because he knew Sarah was planning to open her house early. Or would he?

"Say you nothin'. Saw wood."

With that sibylline utterance, Lomax bowlegged himself off to the tomato plants. Jofferty wrote out a receipt for the Bilbao looking glass on a page from his notebook and asked Max to wrap the thing up for him real good so's it wouldn't get busted. Breaking a mirror that valuable would mean a darn sight more than seven years' bad luck and he'd been getting enough flak about the robberies as it was.

"I'll go over the lists of stolen property as soon as I get back to the station," he promised, "and let you know if I turn up anything. Bilbao looking glass, eh?"

"Sometimes they spell it Bilboa," Max told him. "Means the same thing. Except in Bilbao, of course. Got any cardboard and wrapping paper, Sarah?"

"Bring it into the kitchen. I'll see what I can find."

Wrapping bundles is always more of a

23

nuisance than it starts out to be, and the looking glass presented special problems. Eventually, though, they found enough padding and stiffener to assure a safe ride in the cruiser.

"There you are, Sergeant." Max personally carried the package out and stowed it in the cruiser's trunk. "I've marked it fragile, but you'd better make sure they understand down at the station that it really is. And for God's sake, don't let anybody take off the wrappings."

"They won't get a chance," Jofferty assured him. "We've got a special box down at the bank where we store valuables, and it just so happens I'm the man in charge. I'm going to take this thing directly there and forget to file a report. That satisfy you? Hey, and give my regards to your folks."

As he turned the ignition key in his mud-spattered criser, he glanced over at the magnificent car beside him, and grinned. "Guess your mother must have said more or less the same things mine did when I quit the fish cake factory to join the force. I told her getting shot at now and then's a better deal than spending the rest of my life gutting pollock. See you around, Max. So long, Mrs. Kelling."

"Fine thing," Sarah pouted after he'd driven off. "If Sergeant Jofferty starts calling you Max after he's known you for about thirty seconds, why can't he call me Sarah?"

No doubt he would have, if she were Mrs. Bittersohn instead of Mrs. Kelling. No matter how far he'd stretched his roots, Max would always be accepted around the North Shore in a way none of her own crowd would ever be, even though they'd been trooping here summer after summer, some of them for three and four generations. Lines between summer people and year-rounders might be less sharply drawn these days than they were in her grandparents' time, but they still existed and it wasn't fair.

"You're a bunch of snobs, that's what. Look at you. You don't even come from Ireson Town and everybody treats you like his long-lost cousin. Even with Alexander, they never — "

She stopped short. Max must be getting awfully fed up with Alexander by now. "Come upstairs and help me wrestle with the new mattresses. Mr. Lomax has got them in the wrong rooms."

They were busy putting the guest room

25

THE JEFFERSON-MADISON
REGIONAL PUBLIC LIBRARY
CHARLOTTESVILLE, VA.

to rights when the telephone rang. Sarah had a pillow jammed under her chin and was struggling to cram it into a case that must have shrunk in the wash. "Answer that, will you, Max?" she mumbled. "It's probably your pal Jofferty about the looking glass. Maybe he's found out where it belongs."

Max ran to the phone, but was back upstairs before Sarah had got the second pillowcase unfolded. "It's for you. Some woman named Tergoyne. She thought she'd got the wrong number."

"Couldn't you have convinced her she had?"

Sarah was not panting to chat with, or rather listen to, Miffy Tergoyne. Miffy was one of the old yacht club set to which Alexander's parents had once belonged. Their official membership had been dropped after Alexander's father died and his yacht had to be sold, but the Kellings automatically continued to count as part of the crowd because they always had.

Having become a much gossiped-about widow and, worse, a near-bankrupt one in the past months, Sarah had been counting on social ostracism from the yacht club set as a fringe benefit. Either Miffy was too old to change her ways, though, or else the fact that Sarah was now in possession of her father's relatively modest bequest must have reinstated her among the elect. Well, it couldn't be helped.

Somebody had once observed that the true Boston Brahmin has customs but no manners. Like most generalizations, that remark was probably based on a few unfortunate particulars. One particular could have been Miffy Tergoyne.

"Sarah." Her nasal shriek was enough to cut the phone wires. "Who was that man?"

"Max Bittersohn, my tenant," Sarah told her.

"My God, you're not starting that stuff out at Ireson's? Alice told me but I couldn't believe it, not after Alex. Are you really having an affair with him?"

"How kind of you to take an interest in my affairs," Sarah replied sweetly.

"Is that supposed to be an answer?"

"What makes you think you're entitled to one?"

That actually stopped Miffy, though only for a moment. At last she sniffed and growled, "I must say you've changed."

"No I haven't. This is the first time you've ever bothered to listen to anything I had to say, that's all. To what do I owe the honor, Miffy?"

"I want you and Appie here for drinks at half-past five."

"Sorry, but Aunt Appie's not coming until Monday."

Miffy cackled. "That's what you think, little girl! I phoned Appie this morning and bullied her into starting right away. She ought to be rolling up that god-awful driveway of yours any minute now."

"Miffy, you didn't! I haven't even got the house ready. Did you ever once in your life give any thought to minding your own business?"

"Don't be absurd. Why should I? At half-past five, sharp on the dot. Bring your boy friend. Alice and I want to look him over."

Max came downstairs in time to see Sarah hurl the receiver back on its hook.

"What's the matter?"

"Oh, nothing," she raged, "except that Aunt Appie's about to breeze in here without a word of warning and Miffy expects us all for drinks at five-thirty on the dot. You included."

"Damn it, Sarah, I thought you and I were going to have a few days to ourselves."

"So did I, but that doesn't cut any ice with Miffy."

"Couldn't you simply have told her to go to hell?"

"I did, but she wouldn't listen. It's not Miffy, Max. The real problem is Aunt Appie. I couldn't bear to have her find out she's not welcome. You'll know why when you meet her. Aunt Appie's the eternal Girl Scout, doing her good deed every day and getting kicked in the teeth for it more often than not.

"You never met my Uncle Samuel, a fact for which I hope you're duly grateful. He was the world's most dedicated hypochondriac. Aunt Appie nursed him through every disease in the medical book. At last he died of a misprint and I truly believe she's sorry he's gone.

"When Cousin Dolph told her I was coming out here for the summer and came up with the bright idea that she ought to come too, because the change would do her good, I wanted to slaughter them both but I hadn't the heart to tell her she couldn't come. Aunt Appie tried so hard to ease things for Alexander all those years when he was stuck with taking care of his mother."

There she went again. Max was looking

thunderous, and no wonder. Sarah flung her arms around his neck. "I'll make it up to you somehow. I promise."

"That's what you say," he grumbled.

However, he was still allowing himself to be placated when they heard the taxi from the railroad station clattering over the potholes outside. With her fingers, Sarah hastily rubbed lipstick off Max's chin.

"Don't you dare go sneaking off. You'll have to meet her sometime."

"How long's she going to be around, for God's sake?"

"I have no idea. Not long, most likely. She's not going to be all that comfortable, you know, with half the furniture up in Boston and no heat but the fireplace. You know how raw it can get at night here so close to the water. Oh dear, I do hope Mr. Lomax remembered to have the chimney swept. I don't know what the High Street Bank would do to me if I let the place burn down."

Sarah's property was under litigation because of a disputed mortgage. The big house itself wasn't worth much, unless some enterprising architect wanted to spend a few hundred thousand dollars converting it into luxury condominiums. The thirty-

single thing except visit your friends and enjoy yourself. And Max is not the odd-job man, so don't get any bright ideas about having him paint the house or build you a kayak."

"Sarah, you do get the oddest notions. Whatever would I do with a kayak? But then how do we manage the trash?"

"Mr. Lomax comes with his truck and takes it away, the same as he's always done. He also copes with the repairs, the grounds, and the garden. I'm going to be weeding the vegetables and Max will attend to his own business. We'll all three be awfully busy, so you'll have to amuse yourself with Miffy and the yacht club bunch. They'll keep you hopping, never fear. Now come upstairs and let's get you settled."

"Just let me fill my lungs with this wonderful air first. Umaah!"

There were two kinds of Kellings, the longs and the shorts. The tall ones inclined to oblong faces and eagle-beak noses. A few, like Sarah's late husband, had managed to be handsome. Most did not.

The short Kellings had squarish faces, straight little noses, and mouths that could be described, though never by Kellings themselves, as kissable. Their contours were gentle, ranging from agreeably curved to much too fat. Sarah herself was an unusually pleasant specimen of the shorts.

Aunt Appie, also a Kelling-Kelling like Sarah since the Kellings tended to marry their distant cousins and keep the money in the family, was a long; one of the scraggy longs. As she stood snuffling up the salt air with arms outstretched and nostrils flaring, she might have inspired Cyrus Dallin's "Appeal to the Great Spirit" if she'd had a horse under her and been wearing moccasins and breechclout instead of sensible oxfords and a green seersucker shirtwaist that actually did suggest a Girl Scout uniform.

Having primed her pumps, Appie led the march into the house, lugging a bulging photograph album she intended to entertain Sarah with during the long, cozy evenings. Max who'd had other ideas about how to beguile the moonlight hours, eyed the album without favor.

"Your room isn't ready because I wasn't expecting you until Monday," Sarah told her aunt. "Max and I just got here ourselves. I'm not even unpacked yet, and neither is he."

"Then we'll all bustle around at once and get ourselves stowed away shipshape and

Bristol fashion. What fun! Shoo, chickens. Old mother hen will build her own nest and lie in it with the greatest of ease. Oh, she floats through the air — "

Even Max couldn't help grinning as they left Appie thumping pillows and rattling drawers. "I see what you mean," he murmured. "Is she always like that?"

"Pretty much. Just be firm with her if she offers to cook you anything or starts organizing an expedition to study the tufted titmouse in its native habitat. Some of her old pals will be wanting her to go and stay with them, God willing, as soon as they find out she's in town. You are going to drive us to Miffy's, I hope? Aunt Appie would be heartbroken if she thought you were being left out of the general jollity."

"Will there be any?"

"It'll be deadly. The interesting people stay clear of Miffy. But Aunt Appie will enjoy herself. All we have to do is get her nicely planted at the party, then sneak off alone. Once they've all poured a few of Miffy's martinis down the hatch, they won't know who's there and who isn't."

"Then how's she going to get back here?"

"Somebody will bring her, sooner or later. Don't look so glum, darling. We'll work things out one way or another. Come and see your new home. I hope the paint's dry."

Despite her resolution not to spend any money on the Ireson's Landing place until she knew whether or not she still owned it, Sarah had done a fair amount of titivating in the carriage house. She'd had to. The little apartment over the stalls hadn't been occupied by a coachman since 1915, and the cobwebs practically had to be hacked through with a machete.

She and Mr. Lomax had brushed and scrubbed the walls and ceiling, then covered the old gray plaster with creamy yellow paint. The exposed beams had been oiled with some magic potion brewed by Mr. Lomax, the battered furniture painted bright red and camouflaged as far as possible with India print throws and cushions. The wide-board pine floor, which was really beyond restoration, had been painted dark green and covered by a braided rug Mrs. Lomax had made some time ago. Mrs. Lomax was laid up with arthritis now, but still pleased to be doing something for Isaac Bittersohn's boy because she'd always thought a heap of Isaac.

There wasn't much they could do about

the old-fashioned bathroom except clean it. As to the kitchen, there wasn't one. Max would take his meals at the big house or, if Kellings got too thick on the ground, go over to Miriam or his mother for a handout.

Sarah hadn't got to meet Max's parents yet. Apparently that wasn't going to happen until she was ready to affirm without a qualm or a sniffle that she was ready to tie the knot. She wished she were. It would be so much pleasanter to share these two bright rooms with Max than to rattle around with Aunt Appie in that drafty ark on top of the hill. She gave him a rather forlorn smile and went back to finish her own settling-in.

CHAPTER 3

"Well, Sarah, you're looking a shade less bedraggled than you did the last time I saw you, though I don't suppose you'll ever get over losing Alex. Too bad you never managed to have a child. That would have been some consolation, though probably not much the way they're all turning out these days. What in God's name do you think Miffy put in these martinis?"

"I wouldn't know."

Sarah refrained from wishing it were something instantly lethal, and wriggled herself away from Pussy Beaxitt. Max, she noticed, had been cornered by somebody wanting a free appraisal of what was alleged to be a Rembrandt Peale but most likely wasn't. She trusted he wouldn't be foolish enough to oblige. She ought to have had brains enough not to drag him here in the first place. She'd forgotten how unspeakably god-awful these gatherings of Miffy's could be.

A year ago, she'd have been passively bored instead of actively hating every second she spent here. She'd got used to boredom ages ago, since that had seemed her inescapable lot. First she'd been only Walter Kelling's daughter, too young to count with the grown-ups and too shy to mingle with any teen-agers who might be around. Then, about the time she might have been making her debut and perhaps arousing a little interest among the stag line, her father had died from eating poisoned mushrooms and she'd married the distant cousin Walter had named as Sarah's guardian. As Alexander's wife she'd never got much attention either. Who'd notice quiet little Sarah when they'd always had to take her mother-in-law, the beautiful, blind, intelligent, opinionated Caroline Kelling, with them?

But she wasn't little Sarah any more. Sudden widowhood and unexpected crises had pushed her out of the old rut; a long way out but still not far enough or she wouldn't be here now, nursing a glass of the vermouth that hadn't got put into the martinis and wondering why she hadn't had guts enough to be rude to Pussy.

Aunt Appie was enjoying herself, at any rate. She had one of Miffy's awful cocktails in her hand and was sipping at it with every appearance of relish as she entertained a cluster of her chums with a groan-by-groan replay of Uncle Samuel's final illness. She'd be regaled in turn with cozy details about how other members of the old guard had expired in agony or wasted silently away as the case might have been. She'd be showered with invitations to this, that, and the other thing; and nobody would be crushed to learn her niece Sarah was too busy to accompany her.

Sarah only hoped Appie was bearing in mind the fact that they had no car to provide taxi service. She knew how Cousin Lionel would feel about using up costly gasoline ferrying his mother around to her routs and revels; and Sarah wasn't about to let Max get roped into driving Appie.

Between being a dumping-ground for the whole Kelling tribe's problems and a seeing-eye dog for his mother, Alexander had wound up having time for everybody except his wife. That wasn't going to happen with the next man she married. Anyway, Max didn't show any particular inclination to become a universal father-figure. She thought about what Max wanted and blushed, since after all she'd led a sheltered life in some respects.

"Been out in the sun, Sarah?"

For a moment, Sarah couldn't place this tall man with the weather-beaten face and the sun-bleached hair. Then she decided he must be a Larrington. Hadn't somebody mentioned a while ago that one of the twins had got divorced? Would that be Fren or Don? Anyway, this ought to be Fren because Don always wore his Porcellian tie even, rumor had it, in the shower.

"Hello, Fren," she replied, taking a chance on getting it right. "No, I haven't been at Ireson's long enough for sunning. It must be windburn from all the hot air that's blowing around in here. Why aren't you out on your boat?"

"She's having her bottom scraped."

"Sounds painful. I hope she's not minding too much."

"I am. My God, Sarah, do you know what it costs to maintain a boat these days?"

"No, and don't tell me. I know far too well what other things cost."

"Oh, right. Alex left you strapped, didn't

he? Must have been quite a jolt. Understand you've been running a boarding house or some damn thing to keep body and soul together. You'll drop that, of course, now that you've got your hands on Walter's money."

"Why should I? It's fun and it pays the taxes."

"But Jesus, why a boarding house? Bunch of God-knows-whats all over the place."

"They're hardly a bunch of God-knows-whats," Sarah informed him rather snappishly. "I have Cousin Brooks and his wife, old Mrs. Gates from Chestnut Hill, an accountant who works for Cousin Percy, and one of Mrs. LaValliere's granddaughters."

Fren shrugged. "Miffy got it wrong then, as usual. She told me you had a houseful of Jews from Lynn or Chelsea."

"Just one, and he's from Saugus." Sarah was not about to let Fren Larrington see how furious she was. "That's Max Bittersohn over there by the door. The intelligent-looking one."

Max, in a light blazer jacket and well-pressed flannels, did make an agreeable contrast to the hairy bare legs and dirty Topsiders around him. Other women were noticing, too. Sarah was not surprised to see the expressions on their faces, though it was a bit of an eye-opener to observe who some of the women were.

Max must be used to mass adulation by now. At any rate, he was wearing the polite, fixed smile that told Sarah he was bored already and wondering how he'd let himself get sucked into coming. So was she. While Fren maundered on about jib booms and backstays, Sarah stood wondering how soon they could decently make their escape. She'd just about decided it would be inhumane to keep Max there one moment longer when Alice B. whizzed in with a trayful of something hot and no doubt exotic.

She always moves as though she'd been wound up and set going, Sarah thought. She herself could just about remember when Alice B., as in Toklas, had come to live with Miffy. One or two of the literati among the group had tried calling Miffy Gertrude, as in Stein, but that hadn't ever worked. Miffy was Miffy and that was that.

Nobody really knew or very much cared what precise relationship existed between Miffy and Alice B. So-called Boston marriages between women of independent means who either didn't like men or couldn't get men to like them had been common enough long before their time. Miffy'd always gone in for cropped hair and egomania, while Alice B. took naturally to arty clothes and fancy cooking, at which latter she was in fact extremely good. Aunt Appie was already taking large bites out of whatever Alice B. had concocted this time and exclaiming "Supermella gorgeous!"

But Max wouldn't agree, Sarah realized as soon as she'd got one of the things herself and bitten through puff pastry into a filling of chopped clams and whipped cream. Max hated shellfish and shied away from rich foods of any sort. She must warn him. Alice B. would throw a public fit if he were to take one taste and leave the rest uneaten. When Bradley Rovedock came in and Fren turned to complain to him about the exorbitant cost of bottom-scraping, she grabbed the chance to slip away and cross the room.

She was sorry not to have a word with Bradley, whom she'd always liked, but there was no time to lose. Alice B. was now in among the women surrounding Max, dispensing her clam tarts, twitching her sharp little nose this way and that, sniffing out whatever might be going on for eager speculation and early repetition.

Alice B. never forgot a face, a name, or an indiscretion. Though she'd wait for the most awkward possible moment to share what she'd learned or deduced, she was never stingy about passing it on. Nor did it ever occur to her that she might have heard or guessed wrong. It was no doubt Alice B. and not Miffy who'd come up with the houseful of God-knew-whats from Lynn. When she got face-to-face with Max, she turned up her round, black birds' eyes and gave him a long, thoughtful stare. Then she crowed.

"I know you. You're the Bittersohn boy. Whatever happened to that girl you were living with? Becky, was it? Or Bertha?"

Sarah noticed Max's jawbones tighten, but he answered calmly enough. "Her name was Barbara. The last I heard, she was in Switzerland."

"What was she doing there?"

"I wouldn't know."

This was a bit much. Sarah had to step in.

"I'll bet you don't know what time it is, either," she said. "Come on, Max. You promised to have me back at the house by six o'clock."

45

"Why?" Alice B. demanded.

Sarah ignored her. Max set down his barely touched drink.

"Is your aunt coming with us?"

"I expect she'd like to stay on for a while. You'll see that she gets a ride when she's ready, won't you, Alice B.? Thanks for the clam tart. It was delicious."

"Your friend Mr. Bittersohn didn't get one."

Alice B. was still blocking the way with her depleted tray. Sarah took one of the few remaining pastries and slipped neatly around her.

"He can eat it on the way. I really do have to rush. Say goodbye to Miffy for me."

They got out of the house and into the car without speaking another word to each other. After they'd driven away from the village, Sarah opened her window and threw the tart into the bushes.

"The skunks will enjoy it," she observed. Even to herself, her voice sounded as if she were slowly strangling.

"All right, I know what you're thinking," Max snarled back.

"It's just that I'd rather have heard it from you than from Alice B. Not that it's any of my business, of course."

"Don't be so damned polite! I'd have told you months ago if I'd thought it mattered to us. I haven't seen Barbara in twelve years, for God's sake."

"And how — " No, she couldn't ask him that.

She didn't have to. Max knew, as always. He pulled off the road and stopped the car.

"We might as well have it out right now, Sarah, and get it over with. Okay, in my business I'm bound to meet a few bored rich women who think they've hired a stud instead of an investigator. Since you want to know, they haven't. I don't screw around with my clients or my clients' wives. That's not how I operate. The same thing goes for my suspects because I'm not a damn fool. That's not to say I've been any plaster saint like your darling Alexander."

"Let's leave Alexander out of this, Max. You don't have to tell me anything you don't want to."

"The hell I don't. What kind of an earful do you think that woman's giving your crowd back there about me right now?"

"I couldn't possibly care less about the crowd back there."

"Your aunt's among them, isn't she?"

"Aunt Appie never believes anything bad about anybody."

"In a pig's eye she doesn't. I suppose you don't, either. Go ahead, tell me you're not wondering what the hell you've got yourself into."

"I haven't got myself into anything."

"That's right. You haven't, have you?"

"Max, it's not on account of you. I've explained over and over. It's — all right, tell me about this Barbara if it will make you feel better. Who was she?"

"A graduate student I met at B.U. while I was finishing my doctorate. She was taking a master's in art history so we naturally kept bumping into each other."

"Then it was some time ago."

"I told you that."

"Oh, stop being an idiot. Exactly how old were you?"

"Twenty-three."

"Wasn't that awfully young to be finishing your doctorate?"

"I'd been working my ass off, if you want to know. I had to have that degree."

"You'd already started your business then?"

"Yes, in a small way. That was how Barbara and I got together. She had a part-time job in one of the galleries on Newbury Street and a little apartment over it that she shared with another student. I happened to do some work for the gallery and she'd invite me up for a drink when she saw me there. One thing sort of led to another."

Max was not enjoying this. "Anyway, after a while her roommate moved out and I moved in. I'd got my doctorate by then and was able to work full-time. I made enough to pay the rent and buy the groceries, so Barbara quit her job, which paid peanuts anyway, and started helping me. She'd line up appointments, send out bills, keep track of expenses, do a little research, take a lot of the details off my hands so that I could take on more assignments. She was bright, she had the right sort of training and some contacts from the gallery. And she was crazy about me. Boy, was she crazy about me."

His lips twisted. "So there we were, tripping hand in hand down life's highway with me wondering when I'd be able to scrape together a couple of extra bucks for the license and Barbara telling me it didn't matter because ours was the true union of soul and spirit and how about dinner at the Ritz because we couldn't afford to get married."

"I must say that solution wouldn't have occurred to me," Sarah remarked because she had to give him a moment's relief somehow.

"What was I supposed to do?" he snapped back. "That was the way she wanted it, and I was in no position to do anything else at the time. Anyway, things went along fairly well for a while. With Barbara carrying part of the load, I managed to land a few decent assignments. Then I got my once-in-a-lifetime chance. I got wind of this very personable man-about-town type who whiled away his idle hours contacting rich collectors and persuading them to donate their spare works of art to museums and colleges so they could claim big tax deductions. He got a small percentage for acting as go-between."

"But Max, that's perfectly legitimate, isn't it? I know Cousin Percy gave a Bierstadt to the Worcester museum, and nobody minded except Cousin Mabel."

"Yes, but I expect the Bierstadt your cousin gave was the Bierstadt the museum got. The way this other guy handled the deal, the donors would claim deductions for the full value of the originals but the donees would find out sooner or later they'd been landed with fakes. That created some very embarrassing situations. The original owners were afraid of getting tagged for conspiracy to defraud the government even though they'd acted in perfectly good faith. The museums were naturally teed off at not getting what they'd been led to expect, but didn't dare squawk too loudly for fear of being made to look like fools and antagonizing other potential donors."

"I see. This man was having the paintings copied, palming off the copy with the provenance of the original attached to it, and then keeping the original for his own purposes. Sounds familiar."

"Yes, it's an old trick but it still works if you work it right. This man was a master. So I decided to take on the case as a gamble, hoping to get back my expenses from some of the people who'd been defrauded and figuring it would be the right sort of advertising for me if I could pull it off. I spent a lot of time and money I couldn't afford chasing down leads and piling up evidence, with Barbara right in there pitching every step of the way. She even bought us a second-hand safe to store the evidence in."

He fell silent again. "And then what?" Sarah prodded.

"And then, just as I was ready to spring my trap, Barbara opened the safe, took out the evidence, and handed it to my man as a wedding present. They spent their honeymoon in Zurich. At least I assume they did. That was on the postmark of the envelope she mailed back to me, containing the key to the empty safe."

"Oh, Max! What did you do?"

"What could I do? Cursed myself for a jerk and went back to the nickel-and-dime stuff so I could pay up some of my back bills. Since then, I haven't had a roommate. Satisfied?"

He reached over to the ignition key, and started the motor.

CHAPTER 4

They might have worked out the situation between them if Appie Kelling had stayed at the party half an hour longer. Max had got a fire going to stave off the evening chill. Sarah had fixed two drinkable whiskies and the simple cheese-and-cracker snack Max liked best. They were just settling themselves to talk it over when Appie blew in.

"Yoo-hoo, kiddies. Are you there? Ah, a driftwood fire, how delightful! And look what I've brought."

What she'd brought stepped forward somewhat diffidently. "Hello, Sarah. Forgive me for crashing the party. I didn't get a chance to speak to you at Miffy's, so when Appie invited me in, I couldn't resist."

"Bradley, how nice. It has been ages."

Sarah's greeting was a shade warmer than

it might have been if she hadn't been so annoyed by his being dragged in at such a time, and if Max hadn't been looking so thunderous. Anyway, like it or not, she was about to have that chat with Bradley Rovedock she'd missed at Miffy's.

Bradley was just about Alexander's age. They'd fished, sailed, gone crabbing together as boys, and kept up an agreeable acquaintance though not a close friendship forever after. Bradley'd been one of the few who'd bothered to talk with young Sarah at those sticky gatherings where she'd always felt so out of place. The occasional day cruises on his yacht *Perdita* had been glittering highlights of her summers at Ireson's.

"I've been wanting to see you, Sarah. I hadn't known about Alex and Caro. I've just got back, you see."

He didn't say any more about that, but simply took the hand she held out to him. "You're doing all right now, though? You look quite lovely, if I may say so."

"Thank you, Bradley. You're looking well, too." Bradley always did, of course. "Have you met my tenant, Max Bittersohn? He's taken my carriage house for the summer."

Why did she have to say that? Couldn't she simply have introduced Max as himself?

54

He'd stood up to shake hands with Bradley, but Sarah could tell he was having to strain to act civil. Well, why shouldn't he? She wasn't having any picnic either.

How could she have known she was innocently leading Max to the slaughter at Miffy's? It wasn't him Alice B. had deliberately been trying to embarrass; Alice B. wouldn't give a rap for the Bittersohn boy. It was Sarah she'd been out to get, as he might have had sense enough to realize. Not that Sarah cared about Max's having lived with another woman before he'd met her. Why should she? She herself had been living with another man, hadn't she?

But that had been different. All right, she was jealous. Jealous of that female freebooter who'd been making love to young Max Bittersohn in an apartment over an art gallery while demure little Sarah Kelling sat minding her manners and being ignored at Miffy Tergoyne's awful parties. Jealous of that Barbara who'd done as she liked and taken what she wanted and didn't mind whether or not she wrecked the life of the man she'd pretended to be crazy about. And landed Sarah Kelling years later with yet another mess to straighten out. Damn Barbara!

And damn Max for not having let her know

before that he'd been made a fool of by a woman on the take. He knew how Alexander had suffered in silence all those years for having committed the same sort of mistake, and how Sarah had been made miserable too because Alexander had thought it his duty to protect her from the awful truth. And damn Aunt Appie for — no, it wasn't fair to damn Appie Kelling for being Appie. Damn Sarah herself for being so gutless and witless that she couldn't think of a civil way to make these two nice people go away so she could give Max Bittersohn the straightening-out he damn well needed.

At least Appie was so full of her visit among her cronies that there was no need for Sarah to attempt making conversation. Appie kept appealing to Bradley when she couldn't remember the details, which was most of the time. He filled her in as best he could with that agreeably offhand manner Sarah remembered so well, as if it weren't a bore for him but a courtesy to which Appie was naturally entitled and which he was happy to accord.

Sarah, who at least knew the people they were talking about, managed to put in a comment often enough not to seem rude. Max hardly uttered a word. When Appie started pressing Bradley to stay and take potluck with them, Sarah wasn't surprised to see Max get up and set his empty glass on the mantel with a controlled force that suggested he'd rather have hurled it into the fireplace.

"Nice to have met you, Rovedock," he said with a curt nod.

"But you're not going?" Appie cried. "I took it for granted you'd be dining with us. Really, it won't be a speck of trouble. I'll just pop my casserole into the oven."

"Aunt Appie, you'll do nothing of the sort." Sarah hoped she hadn't screamed, but suspected she had. "I told you before, you're here as a guest."

"Sarah dear, I was only — "

"Trying to be useful. I know. When I want help I shan't hesitate to ask for it. Until I do, you're not to volunteer. Fix her drink, Bradley, and tell her to behave herself. Max, shall I keep something hot for you or leave a snack in your room?"

"Don't bother. I'll grab something. Enjoy your dinner."

He was gone. Aunt Appie's flood of trivia swelled behind him. Sarah went out to the kitchen and slammed the tuna fish casserole into the oven.

Perhaps Bradley was perceptive enough

to have noticed there were undercurrents. When Appie had to go upstairs for, as she girlishly put it, personal reasons, he took the opportunity to remark to Sarah, "I hope my staying hasn't upset your domestic arrangements."

"I haven't had time to make any," Sarah replied. "Max and I just got here this afternoon. I wasn't expecting Aunt Appie till next week, but Miffy got the bright idea of calling her up and hurrying her along before I'd even unpacked my toothbrush. For goodness' sake don't let Aunt Appie realize what a pickle she's put me in by coming too early. She'd either slink back to Cambridge in tears or else foul everything up even worse than it is now by pitching in and trying to help. Right now I couldn't cope with either."

"Poor little Sarah. I hate having to think of your being forced to cope with anything. It bothers me dreadfully that I wasn't around when I might have been of some use to you."

Sarah didn't care to dwell on what might have been. "Where were you this time?" she asked him. "The Galapagos Islands?"

He smiled. "No, I hardly think I'd care to venture that far in a thirty-six footer. I've been puttering around down among the Bahamas and the Antilles, mostly, dodging winter. Gets into an old man's bones, you know."

His smile was somewhat like Alexander's, Sarah thought. He used it oftener, but then Bradley Rovedock had a great deal more to smile about. He'd inherited all the money he'd ever need and no encumbrances. Looks and charm weren't exactly rife among the yacht club set, but Bradley had more of both than anybody else in the group, now that Alexander was gone. He had the yachtsman's weathered skin, the bleached-out hair, the wrinkles around the eyes from squinting across open water for hours at a stretch, day after day, year after year. He also had the trim figure and the easy carriage of an outdoorsman. Sarah, who was on her second Scotch and probably shouldn't have been, felt an urge to giggle.

"What's so funny, little Sarah?"

"Nothing really," she told him. "I suspect I'm a wee bit drunk. It was just the idea of your old bones. You'll never change, Bradley."

"Is that a compliment or a criticism?"

"Right now I'd say it's a comfort."

"I'm glad."

He reached over to brush the back of her hand with the tips of his fingers. Then Appie Kelling came downstairs and it was casserole time. After they'd eaten, Bradley took his leave either out of consideration or because he was afraid he'd be offered a second helping.

That was one thing to be said for her aunt's casseroles, Sarah thought as she washed up after the meal. Once word got around that she was making them, nobody else would accept Appie's invitations to take potluck at the Kellings'. Alice B. would pump Bradley tomorrow about what he'd got to eat here, and would draw the correct inference from what he didn't tell her.

Even Appie herself had fallen back on Alice B.'s clam tarts as an excuse to refuse a larger helping. Sarah set the still almost-full baking dish outdoors for some undiscriminating creature of the night to clean for her, and looked down over the knoll to see whether there was a light in the carriage house window yet. No, Max wasn't back. Off interviewing a new female assistant, maybe. Why couldn't he have told her?

Because he was still hurt over Barbara's desertion, she supposed. Men were like that. Crammed things down where they wouldn't show, and pretended they weren't feeling the misery. Women knew enough to cry and complain and make scenes. Sarah felt like making one now.

A fat lot of good it would do her. Aunt Appie would start crashing around with hot milk and mustard plasters or some other abominations and Max wouldn't even know because he was somewhere else with God knew whom.

Maybe he didn't mix sex with business, as he claimed, but Sarah didn't believe for one second that he'd gone celibate ever since Barbara had run out on him. Maybe he hadn't been suffering quite so much as he'd complained about these past few months while he'd allegedly been pining for young widow Kelling to quit grieving after what she'd never had in the first place.

Sarah was no fool. She realized now that what she couldn't let go of was the might-have-been that never was, the marriage that had lasted seven years without ever becoming a real marriage at all. Alexander had been too overwhelmed by those misfortunes he'd never talked about to get around to the things people were presumed to marry for. Sarah could have had an affair herself, she supposed. Alexander probably would never have noticed and wouldn't have blamed her much if he had.

But she hadn't, and she wasn't about to have one with Max Bittersohn. Meaningful encounters weren't her sort of thing, nor was that what Max himself wanted. Now she could understand why he was so insistent on getting the knot firmly tied. Or had been, until tonight. Could any man's ardor survive the kind of summer this was starting out to be?

Sarah couldn't blame Max for having walked out on Aunt Appie and Bradley Rovedock. If she'd had brains enough, she might have thought up an excuse to go with him. Assuming he'd have wanted her. Maybe all Max needed was a chance to be by himself for a while to think things out. As to what he might be thinking she'd better not speculate if she expected to get any sleep tonight. Sarah went back into the house, finished straightening the kitchen, then sat down with Aunt Appie and the family photograph album.

CHAPTER 5

Long after Aunt Appie had yawned herself off to bed, Sarah stayed downstairs, doing the chores she hadn't been able to get at earlier, casting glances over at the carriage house far oftener than she meant to. The outside light stayed on, and the inside remained dark. At last she gave up and went to bed.

The new mattress was sublime, the sound of waves breaking against the cliff ought to have been lulling. It was a long time, though, before Sarah got to sleep and still she hadn't heard any car come up the drive. She woke later than she'd meant to, and then only because Appie Kelling was poking a sloppy cup of lukewarm tea under her nose.

"Surprise!" Appie caroled. "I was up with the birds, communing with the gulls and the terns. Such a glorious morning. Now you lie there and drink your tea, dear. I'll pop down to the kitchen and whip us up a batch of pancakes."

"No you won't." How Appie always managed to burn something as thin as a pancake to a black crust outside while leaving it raw in the middle was a mystery Sarah had never been able to unravel, nor had she any desire to be faced with it this morning.

"Cousin Theonia sent a gorgeous coffee ring that has to be eaten before it goes stale. Anyway, the kitchen is off limits to everybody but me. That's captain's orders, Aunt Appie. You'd better remember, or I'll send a squadron of gulls to bombard you with clamshells. Is that the telephone ringing? Go answer it since you're champing to be useful. If it's for me, ask them to hold on a minute."

"Aye aye, captain."

Delighted to be of service, any service, Appie sped away. Sarah made a quick trip to the bathroom, splashed cold water over her face because there wasn't any hot and wouldn't be until she broke down and lit the heater, then threw on her old corduroy slacks and a sweater, for the morning was still crisp.

As she ran downstairs, she wondered whether the phone call was from Max. Since last January, when he'd begun occupying her basement room on Tulip Street, she'd gotten used to having him leave the house without fanfare, then call up from Mexico City or somewhere to say he wouldn't be in to dinner. He'd told her he had nothing urgent on at the moment, but that didn't mean he hadn't thought of something by now. Aunt Appie wasn't making any noises about calling her to the phone, though. When she got downstairs, Appie clapped a hand over the mouthpiece and hissed, "It's Miffy."

That was a relief. Miffy must be after Appie to come over for luncheon and bridge or something. Sarah dodged into the kitchen and began filling the coffeepot. She couldn't get a clear view of the carriage house from here on account of the sloping ground and the trees between, but she did manage to notice that the outside light had been switched off, and thought she caught a glimpse of his car through the leaves.

No sense waiting breakfast for him. The kitchen clock Mr. Lomax had wound up and set going for her said only half-past eight. Early rising was not Max's forte at any time, and heaven only knew what time he'd blown in last night. He'd straggle along sooner or later, unless he was still in a snit.

Maybe she'd saunter down that way after she'd got a cup of coffee into her and lay a wreath of forget-me-nots on the doorstep. But why should she be the peacemaker? It was Max himself who'd — no, it was Alice B. who'd stirred up the trouble between them for the fun of being nasty. If either she or Miffy thought Sarah Kelling was ever going to attend another of their booze-ups, they might as well think again. She was putting Cousin Theonia's elegant coffee cake on the table when Appie came into the kitchen.

"Sarah?"

"Pull up a chair. The coffee's almost ready. I'm just going to — Aunt Appie, what's the matter?"

"That was Miffy."

"Yes, I know. You said so before. What's wrong? Is she sick?"

"It's Alice B. She's dead."

"You don't mean it! But why? She looked fine yesterday. Was it a heart attack?"

"They think it was the axe."

"The what?"

"The axe. From the woodpile, you know.

Miffy and Alice B. always come to Ireson Town so early and leave so late — "

"Aunt Appie, are you saying she went to chop wood for a fire and cut herself so badly that — no, it wasn't that, was it? Somebody — "

"I don't think they actually chopped her up, dear. Not into bits, anyway. Otherwise, Miffy wouldn't have known it was Alice B., would she? Oh, Sarah!"

Not even Appie could go on being bright and cheery about such a horror as this. She sat down at the table and buried her face in the checkered napkin Sarah had laid out for her. Sarah got the whiskey and poured a tot into a juice glass.

"Here, drink this. I'll get you some hot coffee."

"Sarah dear, I don't need — "

"Yes you do. You've had a ghastly shock."

"But what about you?"

"I've grown used to this sort of thing," Sarah told her grimly. "Anyway, you liked Alice B."

"Of course, dear. Everyone did."

"I didn't."

"But Alice B. was so full of fun!"

"Alice B. was a malicious old bitch. Her notion of fun was slipping a dagger between

67

somebody's ribs when they weren't expecting it."

"Sarah, how can you say such a thing?"

"Because it happens to be true. Her getting murdered doesn't make Alice B. any more amiable. It simply removes her as an active menace. I shouldn't wonder if the only person who may honestly feel sorry about this is yourself. And Miffy, I suppose, because now Alice B. won't be around to fetch and carry for her."

"Oh, Sarah."

Appie Kelling took a sip of the coffee Sarah placed before her and automatically murmured, "Delicious. But dear, it's so horrible."

"I'm not saying it isn't. Murder is always horrible, but if anybody ever went looking to be killed, Alice B. did. Hasn't Miffy any idea who may have done it?"

"She could barely talk straight. I must go to her, Sarah. You don't have a bicycle, do you? Or perhaps that young man in the carriage house would — "

"Max Bittersohn? I expect he would, under the circumstances, but I've no idea how late he got in or how long he'll want to sleep. Can't you call one of the crowd? No sense in phoning down for the station taxi. It takes them forever to come. Didn't Miffy give you any details at all?"

"As far as I could gather, she says she came downstairs about five o'clock this morning to get a Bromo Seltzer because she couldn't find any in her upstairs medicine cabinet. She wandered into the dining room for some reason I couldn't make out, and there was Alice B. on the floor in a pool of — "

Appie drank more coffee. "Miffy says it must have been robbery. She couldn't think why else, and there have been so many break-ins."

"Recently?"

"Of course. Why else would they still be talking about them? It seems to me that was all I heard yesterday. Pussy Beaxitt even lost her great-grandmother's horsehair sofa. Can you imagine? She says they drive right up with a moving van and cart the stuff away, bold as brass."

"Did Miffy tell you anything of hers was missing?"

"She was so upset — "

Meaning she was too drunk to make sense, Sarah thought. Faced with a corpse on the floor, Miffy's instinctive reaction would have been to reach for the nearest gin bottle.

"You better had get over there right away," she said aloud. "Miffy's probably not safe to leave alone. Here, eat a slice of coffee cake and drink another cup of coffee. You can't go there on an empty stomach or you'll get sick yourself. While you're having your breakfast, I'll run down to the carriage house and see if Max is awake. Maybe he'll let me take his car and drive you over myself."

"Oh good, then you can stay and help me with Miffy."

"Not on your life. I've too much to do here. Anyway, Max will be wanting his car back."

"But surely, for an old friend like Miffy — "

"Max never met Miffy until yesterday and I doubt very much if he ever wants to see her again."

"Alice B. knew him and that aunt of his or whoever it was he used to live with. I didn't quite catch what they were talking about, but I definitely heard Alice B. say something about a woman named Bertha."

"Did you? Well, I'll go see. Here, let me cut you some more coffee cake. Then maybe you'd better phone Pussy, if she doesn't get to you first. The wires will be

70

humming, I expect."

Actually, Sarah herself could have telephoned down to the carriage house. The old speaking tube that once ran from the kitchen to the coachman's quarters had perished long ago, of course, but Max had got a private phone installed as soon as they'd decided he was to use the apartment. She didn't want to talk to him with Aunt Appie hissing in the background, though, and she'd be silly to pass up an excuse to escape.

It was delicious being out on a morning like this, with the mist still rising from the ground and the wet grass licking at her bare ankles as she ran over the unmown hillside instead of decorously following the path. No doubt she was behaving wretchedly in treating Alice B.'s dreadful death as a personal deliverance, but Sarah had never been one to lie to herself, and she was awfully fed up with having to be sweet to people at the breakfast table.

Especially people who barged into her bedroom and dribbled cups of tea over her neck before she'd got her eyes open. Sarah had meant this to be her special summer, maybe the last one she'd ever get to spend at Ireson's. Already it had begun to go sour, with everyone trying to change her plans for her. Aunt Appie was a dear, but she was also a pest. Having her over at Miffy's instead of underfoot here would be a relief beyond words.

Sarah had reached the carriage house now. She pushed at the outer door and found it unlocked. She ought to remind Max about locking up, she supposed, but what was the sense when there was really nothing down here worth bothering about. The upstairs would be locked, surely. They probably should have put some kind of outside entrance to the apartment, but there wasn't one, just a remarkably fancy staircase with a sawn fretwork casing that ran up from inside what used to be the tack room.

Sarah had always liked coming over here, especially on rainy days when her parents were visiting at the big house and she was the only child in the party. It was a wonderful place to skip rope or bounce a ball. She'd tried sliding down the varished banister once and got splinters in her behind. She'd suffered in silence until they got back to Boston, then asked Cook to take them out rather than confess to her mother and risk being told she couldn't play in the carriage house any more. On the whole, she thought she must have been happier at Ireson's than anywhere else she could remember.

So had Alexander. He'd had the Milburn to dote upon here, for one thing. There'd been firewood to cut and driftwood to gather that made wonderfully colored flames when they'd burned it later in the huge stone fireplace. There'd been wildflowers to find and birds to look at through field glasses that had to be adjusted differently for his eyes and Sarah's because he was so much older than she.

Alexander had known all the birds by their calls, while Sarah couldn't tell them apart unless she managed to sort them out from the foliage and observe the markings on their feathers. She ought to be missing him more out here, but somehow it was working the other way around.

She'd thought of him often enough during these past weeks when she'd been coming out here on the train to spend a day with Mr. Lomax, deciding where to plant the lettuce and the cucumbers, rearranging what was left of the furniture to make a few rooms livable, sneaking an hour off to roam the beach and the headlands.

Even looking out into the ocean from which divers had brought up his mangled body, though, she couldn't feel sad. Alexander had loved the sea. His last day had been perhaps the happiest one of his life, right until the Milburn's brakes had failed and sent him crashing to the rocks below the seawall, with his mother beside him.

Death for the pair of them had been inevitable in any case. Sarah knew that now. She couldn't have done anything to avert the so-called accident because she hadn't known until later why someone had thought it necessary to kill them. Maybe having to stay alive and face what he'd have had to know would have been worse than quick oblivion. Anyway, Alexander was gone and missing him wouldn't bring him back. And here was she and where was Max Bittersohn? She thumped at the upstairs door.

"Max, it's Sarah. Are you there?"

She heard a grunt, then a thud, then the door was open and she was being clasped to a baby-blue pajama front.

"How come you didn't bring the *mishpocheh?*" Max growled into her hair. "Look, you're not sore about last night?"

"Because you ran off and abandoned me to Aunt Appie and the family album?"

74

"You should talk. I got stuck playing cribbage with my Uncle Jake until half-past two."

"I hope he licked the pants off you."

"Took me for seven dollars and forty-two cents. It's all your fault. To what do I owe the honor?"

"I'm here on business, so don't get ideas. Aunt Appie needs a ride over to Miffy Tergoyne's."

"I've been to Miffy's, thanks."

"You don't have to stay. Just drop her off and flee."

"But I'll have to go back and get her?"

"No, she'll be moving in. I don't know for how long." Sarah twisted one of his pajama buttons. "It's another nasty, I'm afraid."

"How nasty?"

"Pretty bad. From what I can gather, a burglar got in last night and killed Alice B. with an axe from their woodpile. Miffy's in a state, as you can well imagine. She needs somebody with her and Aunt Appie needs to be needed so she's anxious to get there before some other angel of mercy beats her to the job. Could you hurry, please?"

"Go tell her to pack her merit badges. I'll be along as soon as I can get my pants on."

CHAPTER 6

Sarah ran back to the house and found, as she might have expected, that Appie was talking on the phone to Pussy Beaxitt. She tapped her on the shoulder.

"Max is on his way. Tell Pussy you'll call her from Miffy's."

Appie, used to peremptory commands from her late husband, obeyed at once. "I've got to go now, Pussy. Sarah's young man is driving me over. Why don't you — oh, you were? Later, then."

She hung up. "Pussy has to go over to the yacht chandler's for some toggle bolts. I think she said toggle bolts. Anyway, she's coming over to Miffy's afterward. Oh Sarah, when I think of poor, dear Alice B. — "

"Do you have everything you need ready to take with you? And did you eat your breakfast?" Sarah was not about to let

Appie get started on poor, dear Alice B. again.

"Yes, dear. All packed and rarin' to go. That prune cake was delicious. I thought you might like to send the rest to Miffy."

"Miffy wouldn't eat it and Max hasn't had his breakfast yet. Nor have I, come to think of it. Anyway, there's sure to be tons of food over there."

Furthermore, Miffy Tergoyne had a lot more money for groceries than Sarah Kelling did, and Aunt Appie was not about to play Lady Bountiful with Cousin Theonia's love-offering. "Make her an eggnog, the way you used to do for Uncle Samuel."

"Oh, how right you are! Dear old Sam always said my eggnogs were the best."

What Uncle Samuel had been wont to say was that Appie's eggnogs were less god-awful than the rest of the slop she fed him, mainly because her generous heart wouldn't allow her to stint on the brandy. Memories, notably Appie Kelling's, could be mercifully deceiving.

"Now Sarah, you mustn't worry. I'll be back in plenty of time so that you won't have to sleep alone here tonight," was Appie's parting shot as she climbed into Max's car. "Aren't you coming with us, just to give Miffy a word of cheer?"

"I have to wait for Mr. Lomax," Sarah lied, "and you mustn't concern yourself for one second about me. There's nothing here a burglar would take as a gift, and Max is handy by. I'm not the least bit nervous, so stay as long as Miffy needs you. Call if you want a change of clothes. Or the family album," she added after the car had started to drive away, and went to pour herself a cup of coffee.

She cast a longing look at Cousin Theonia's coffee cake, but decided it would be cozier to wait and have breakfast with Max. She compromised by cutting herself the merest sliver and carrying that with her coffee out to the side porch, where Mr. Lomax had set out a couple of Adirondack chairs badly in need of paint. Alexander had been intending to scrape and refinish them this summer. He'd enjoyed that sort of fussy job. She'd get around to doing them herself sometime, maybe.

One might ask Pete Lomax, she supposed. Pete was a professional house painter, or alleged to be. He mustn't be overwhelmed with work, since he had so much time to give to his uncle. That was odd, now Sarah thought of it. June was the time of year when homeowners around here were clamoring for painters. Lomaxes were good workers, everybody knew that. Pete seemed able enough, from what little Sarah had seen of him.

Maybe he was helping the elderly care-taker out of the goodness of his heart, but Sarah wasn't inclined to think so. Pete didn't strike her as the sort to go in for self-sacrifice, and there couldn't be anywhere near the money in being assistant to an odd-job man that there was in painting. But then, maybe other people didn't like Pete Lomax any better than she did, so he had trouble getting jobs on his own.

Sarah decided she didn't care to think about Pete Lomax right now. She didn't much want to think about anything. She must be in the grip of what an erudite visitor had once referred to as the thalassal re-gression: that delightful vacuity which takes possession of mind and body during those first few days at the seashore, where noth-ing registers except the sun on one's face, the salt air in one's nostrils, and the pound-ing of surf in one's ears. She couldn't have said whether she'd been sitting on the porch five minutes or an hour when she heard a car taking the drive in low gear.

"Oh, there's Max."

Now she could have another slice of prune cake. It occurred to Sarah that she was hungry. Max must be, too, but what had gone wrong with his car? That sumptuous machine, so lovingly cared for by his brother-in-law's mechanics, had been purring like a kitten when he drove off. A tiger kitten, anyway. Why this chugging and clanking all of a sudden? Because, unfortunately, this wasn't Max's car but Cousin Lionel's old van with his expensively educated troop of juvenile delinquents hanging out the windows and drumming on the sides.

"Where's Mother?" was Lionel's cordial greeting.

"She's gone to take care of Miffy Tergoyne," Sarah snapped back. "They had a robbery last night. Didn't you hear it on the news?"

"I never listen to the news," he replied coldly. "Why can't Alice B. take care of Miffy?"

"Because the robber killed her."

"Yay," shouted his four sons as one voice. "We want to see the body."

"Now see what you've done, Sarah. You know my views on exposing innocent young minds to senseless violence."

Since the innocents were still chanting in unison, "We want to see the body," he had a problem making himself heard.

"When's Mother coming back?"

"Shut up, you little monsters," Sarah shrieked. "Lionel, I have no idea when or whether your mother will be back. She just left. If you want to see her, why don't you go on over to Miffy's? I expect the police have taken the body away by now, but there may be a few bloodstains," she added helpfully.

Lionel got out of the van and slammed the door, perhaps entertaining the fantasy that he'd thereby suppress some of the racket. "Thank you, Sarah. I hope I can do as much for you sometime. I wanted Mother to keep an eye on the boys while I go to see about renting surfboards. Since she isn't here, you'll have to watch them."

"Not on your life. Lionel, if you think I'm going to baby-sit that pack of hyenas now or ever, you've got another think coming. I gave permission for you to camp on my property only because Aunt Appie buttonholed me about it at your fathers funeral and I didn't have the heart to refuse her. Please bear in mind, however, that I don't want you and am not about to tolerate you if you create too much of a nuisance. Now move that heap down the path to the boat-house because I won't have it blocking the drive. You can set up your camp there."

"I prefer to select my own campground, thank you."

"Sorry, but it's the boathouse or no-where. That's the only place you'll be able to get fresh water without pestering me. You may use the toilet there, and the out-door shower. You'll have to pump up the water by hand and be darned careful of that pump because it's on its last legs and Alex-ander's not around any more to fix it. If any of your brats — "

"Sarah, I protest!"

"Yeah, Lionel protests," came the *a capella* chorus from the van.

"Protest all you like, but that's the way it's going to be or you can find yourselves another place to camp. As I started to say, if any of your brats stuffs anything down the john the way they did last time we made the mistake of letting you near the place, you'll have to pay the plumber. You may not, any of you, under any circum-stances, come up to the main house."

"Sarah, this is outrageous," Lionel splut-tered.

"No it's not. I don't yet know whether this property belongs to me or to the High Street Bank. I can't allow it to be damaged for fear they'll slap another lawsuit on me. Furthermore, you're all to stay well away from the carriage house because I've rented it for the season and I won't have my tenant bothered."

"Who's your tenant?" yelled Jesse, oldest and loudest of the tribe.

"That's none of your concern since with any luck at all, he'll never get to meet you. Where's Vare? Why on earth didn't you bring her with you if you knew you had errands to do?"

"Vare's not coming," shouted Woodson, the nine-year-old who was next in line to Jesse. They all had the detestable habit of calling their parents by their first names. "She's gone to be a dyke."

"Don't you mean lesbian, Woody?" his father corrected with the calm detachment required by his advanced views on education. "Vare has decided to explore her homosexual inclinations and has gone to live with Tigger."

"That may be the wisest decision she's ever made," said Sarah.

Marrying Lionel and bearing him four

83

sons in a little under four years in order to gain a richer experience of parenting had undoubtedly been the stupidest, but Vare was like that. Sarah vaguely remembered Tigger as a former college roommate of some cousin or other. She'd lurked on the outskirts at family gatherings sometimes, glaring at anybody who spoke to her and never uttering a word in reply. No wonder Vare was attracted to Tigger.

Sarah couldn't help experiencing some compassion for these four young horrors, but she knew from frightful experience how dangerous it could be to indulge one's higher feelings among this crowd.

"Go back down the drive," she told Lionel as firmly as she possibly could. "Turn left where you see the ruts and follow them along to the boathouse. Mr. Lomax gets in there with his truck all right, so you shouldn't have any trouble with the van. If you get stuck, you're welcome to borrow some shovels and mend the road. That will give you a richer experience of what's involved in keeping up a place like this for the benefit of one's cadging relatives."

Lionel started to say something, evidently decided he hadn't better, and churned off in a belch of blue smoke. Sarah, feeling that she'd won a battle but most likely lost the war, was going back into the house for more coffee when Max at last drove up.

"What the hell did I meet back there?" he asked her.

"Lionel Kelling and his traveling zoo," Sarah answered bitterly. "Aunt Appie's only son, thank God, and his beastly begats. Their mother's gone to be a lesbian."

"Shouldn't she have thought of it sooner? Are they staying here?"

"The idea is that they're to camp down by the boathouse. I've threatened them with everything I could think of if they come up here bothering us, but I don't expect they'll pay any attention."

"Oh well, I don't mind kids."

"You'll mind these," Sarah assured him. "They've been brought up on freedom of expression. Translated, that means Lionel hasn't the guts to be as vicious as he'd like to be, so he's trained the boys to act out his hostilities for him."

"My God. How long are they going to stay?"

"Until I can make them miserable enough to clear out, I suppose. Come on and get something to eat. You must be starved. Did you deliver Aunt Appie all right?"

"Without a hitch. Jofferty was on duty. He sends you his regards."

"I trust you gave him mine in return. Coffee?"

"Please. I can use it."

"Pretty bad over there, was it?"

"More bad than pretty, from what Jofferty told me. They wouldn't let me inside. They'd already taken away the body and sealed off the room where she was found. I was glad of that, for your aunt's sake. Jofferty thinks the killer must have had a personal grudge against the Beaxitt woman, judging from the way she was hacked up."

"Beaxitt? I thought it was Alice B. who got killed."

"Miss Tergoyne's companion, right? Her last name was Beaxitt."

"Good heavens, so it was. I'd completely forgotten Alice B. wasn't just a nickname. She was related somehow or other to Biff Beaxitt, Pussy's husband. That's why Pussy could never stand her. When Biff's mother died, she left Alice B. some hideous garnet jewelry Pussy had set her heart on, though I'll never understand why. Of course Biff's mother loathed Pussy and just did it to spite her. She loathed Alice B., too, I believe, but anyway that's what happened."

"Who gets the jewelry now?"

"If Alice B. ever got around to making a will, I expect it might go to Miffy. If she didn't, I suppose whatever she left would be divided up among the relatives. There are scads of Beaxitts."

"Did this Alice B. have much to leave?"

Sarah paused in the act of cutting more coffee cake. "You know, Max, that's not a bad question. Being a Beaxitt, Alice B. must have had something of her own. They always do. She'd lived off Miffy for years and years, so whatever money she did have must simply have been lying around piling up interest. There could turn out to be a good deal more than one might expect from someone who lived like a sort of poor relation."

"The Tergoyne woman's loaded, right? Suppose she'd been the one murdered instead of the companion. Where would her money go?"

"That's another good question. Miffy's the last of the Tergoynes and she's not into endowing hospitals or that sort of thing. I suppose she'd have left the bulk of it to Alice B. and perhaps some small bequests to old friends. Why? You don't think the killer hacked up Alice B. by mistake? Even in the dark you couldn't get them mixed. Miffy's at least a head taller, and thin as a stick. Alice was a dumpy little thing — you saw her — and those peasant getups she affected made her look even fatter than she was. It couldn't have been all that dark anyway, or whoever swung the axe couldn't have seen where to hit. Have some more prune cake?"

"I'll split a slice with you. On the surface, it appears to have been a rather odd sort of burglary. Jofferty showed me a partial list of the things Miss Tergoyne claims were taken. They're still checking the place over from some kind of inventory list she'd made up for insurance purposes."

Max fished a scrap of paper out of his pocket. "She says she's lost a Fantin-Latour. Where was it? I don't recall seeing one yesterday."

"That's a big house and you were only in the living room. Miffy tends to keep things in unlikely places. If it was a still life, they might have hung it in the kitchen so Alice B. could enjoy it while she chopped the onions."

"And the murderer took it to enjoy while he chopped up Alice?"

"Max, I don't really find that awfully

88

amusing. What else does Miffy say was stolen?"

"This will interest you." Max held out his scribbled list, a fingertip marking the third item down.

"A Bilbao looking glass? Max, you don't think — "

"Jofferty says he asked Miss Tergoyne about that particularly, without explaining why he was so curious. She swears her glass was hanging in the dining room yesterday morning when she and Miss Beaxitt took inventory. He says she told him they went around and checked the entire list every single day. Could she possibly be telling the truth?"

"Knowing Miffy, I shouldn't doubt it for a second," Sarah replied. "She's paranoid about anything that belongs to her, especially since we've had so many robberies around here. She hardly ever leaves her house, except to go south for a month or so during the worst of the winter. When she does, she hires a bonded watchman to stay there, and heaven help the poor soul if there's so much as a box of crackers unaccounted for when she gets back. If Miffy says her Bilbao looking glass was there in the morning, you'd better believe it was.

Otherwise, she wouldn't have been entertaining guests in the afternoon. She'd have been calling out the National Guard and sending telegrams to the Republican party chairman demanding somebody's head on a pike for not having got it back yet. I can't see how the one we found could possibly be hers. But what an odd coincidence."

"Too damned odd," Bittersohn grunted. "I shouldn't have thought Bilbao looking glasses could be that thick on the ground, though I suppose an old seaport like Ireson Town would be as good a place to find them as anywhere. Anything else about that list strike you as peculiar?"

"Well, it's awfully récherché for ordinary burglars, wouldn't you say? They appear to have taken only paintings and objets d'art. No silver, for example, and Miffy has tons of it. And none of the larger pieces like that horsehair sofa they took from Pussy Beaxitt."

She wrinkled her nose in thought. "It seems as if the burglar must have known in advance what was worth stealing and also where to find it, because Miffy kept things in such a jumble. Is that what you wanted me to say?"

"Right on the button. Who in her crowd

would have that kind of expertise?"

"Max, surely you don't — but it would almost have to be, wouldn't it? Unless it was the window cleaner or the rug washer or someone like that. We do get lots of college students doing odd jobs around here during the summer season. Some of them are fairly erudite."

"Do you hire them to help out at parties?"

"Some people do. Miffy doesn't bother since she never serves anything but martinis she makes herself and has Alice B. to take care of the food and the washing-up. Had, I should say. As for her friends — " Sarah hesitated.

"It's hard to say, really. They've all been to private schools and I suppose they got force-fed a certain amount of art history. But they're an awfully dim lot, by and large. Why, Fren," Sarah added unkindly as a gangling form in shorts and sweatshirt manifested itself in her kitchen, "we were just talking about you. I didn't hear you knock. Do you know Max Bittersohn?"

Fren Lamington did not know Max Bittersohn and clearly didn't intend to. He stared straight through the man at the table, turned to the open pantry shelves, found a mug, and helped himself from the coffee-pot.

"Where do you keep the sugar, Sarah? Not a very shipshape galley, I must say."

"Must you? It's none of your business, you know. The sugar's in that canister marked 'Sugar.' Take a clean spoon and don't spill any or we'll have the place overrun with ants. Why aren't you down at the boatyard?"

"Good question."

Fren gulped half the coffee scalding hot and whacked off a hunk of prune cake. "I know I came here for some damn reason or other. Oh yes, dinner at the yacht club. Half-past seven. You'll have to bum a ride from one of the gang. I shan't have time to pick you up. Can't rely on the old Milburn any more, eh?"

It seemed not to occur to Fren that he'd just said something unpardonable. He snatched the last piece of coffee cake from the plate, gulped down the dregs of his coffee, and left without waiting for Sarah to answer.

CHAPTER 7

Sarah got up and hooked the screen door after Fren. She picked up the used mug he'd rudely set on the kitchen table right under Bittersohn's nose, and carried it over to the sink to wash. Then she changed her mind, unlocked the door again, opened it, and hurled the mug as far as she could into the deep grass.

"Now," she said, putting up the hook again, "where were we?"

"We were discussing the quaint social customs of the local fauna," Max replied. "Oh Christ, here's another."

"Miz Alex." That was Pete Lomax bawling through the screen. "The door's stuck."

"No it's not," she told him. "The door is locked because I'm sick and tired of having people barge in without knocking. And I'm Mrs. Kelling, since you appear to have forgotten how to address me. Where's your uncle?"

"He had to go over to Ipswich. Told me to come ahead an' get started. He'll be along pretty soon."

Pete spoke absentmindedly. He was eyeing Max. Sarah decided she might as well explain.

"This is Mr. Bittersohn, who's renting the carriage house and having his meals up here. I hope one of these days he'll be allowed to eat in peace. What do you want, Pete?"

Pete wasn't even listening to her, he was too interested in Max. "Hey, I know you. You used to catch for Saugus High."

"Yes, and I still have the scars on my left leg where you spiked me on purpose after I'd tagged you out trying to steal home," Max replied with no particular animosity. "That was the year we licked you nine to nothing. What's new, Pete?"

"S'pose you heard about Miss Tergoyne's lady friend gettin' bumped off last night?"

Pete lounged up against the door jamb and cast an ever so casual glance at the coffeepot. Jed Lomax would have dropped dead on the spot if he'd arrived here to find his nephew sitting down for a cozy chat

94

with one of his customers. How did one handle this? Sarah decided flight was her best solution.

"If you two are going to hash over old times, I'll get on with my work. Pete, since you're here you may as well get started cutting that grass in the back yard. I told you to do it last week, and the week before."

"Don't you think it looks sort o' pretty the way it is, Miz Kelling?"

The way Pete drawled out the "Miz Kelling" was more than Sarah cared to take. "There's nothing pretty about picking up ticks on one's legs every time one steps outside the door. See that you have it finished by noontime."

At least being a landlady had taught her how to bully people. Sarah stalked out of the kitchen and went upstairs to make beds, wondering whether Pete had ever tried to steal anything other than home plate.

Max might be wondering the same thing. If so, he'd stand a better chance of getting information out of Pete if Sarah wasn't around.

It was strange to picture a Lomax doing anything even mildly reprehensible. Most of them were policemen, firemen, or honest fisher folk. One was a Methodist minister, two were security guards at a college some-where up around Ashby. There was a grandson at Tabor Academy on scholarship and a fair sprinkling of first mates and chief engineers in the merchant marine. Still, any large family was bound to have its black sheep, and Pete looked to Sarah like a plausible candidate.

Maybe she oughtn't to fault him for help-ing his uncle instead of painting houses. Lots of men around here would no doubt welcome the chance to put themselves into a position where they might hope to take over Jed's customers when, if ever, he hung up that old swordfisherman's cap for the last time. Despite its enclaves of wealth, this part of the North Shore was none too affluent by and large. Nor were some of the allegedly wealthy all that rich, as Sarah her-self had reason to know.

It wasn't what Pete did but what he didn't do that bothered her, she thought sourly as she glanced out at the back yard where grass still waved knee-high and the ticks, no doubt, were busy proliferating. Furthermore, she didn't like Pete's manner. She didn't expect to be kowtowed to by the hired help, but neither did she care to be leered at.

Also, while she was on the subject, she didn't go much for being bullied by her old acquaintances. What did Fren Larrington think he was getting at, sailing in and barking orders as though he had some God-given right to take charge now that Alexander wasn't around? Even Cousin Lionel hadn't managed to make himself quite so intolerable in so short a space of time, though to give Lionel his due, he'd tried. He'd just better keep that pack of cubs out of her hair or she might start sharpening the axe herself.

Sarah sat down on the bed she'd just finished straightening, and thought about the dead woman over in the village. What did she actually know about Alice Beaxitt? Nothing much, when she came down to facts, except that Alice B. had managed somehow to live with Miffy a good many years in apparent harmony and that she'd had the most vicious tongue in the yacht club crowd, which was saying a good deal. She'd always seemed more or less the same, got up in some outfit she'd picked up at the shops around Bearskin Neck, always trying out some exotic recipe and trying to make you eat more of it than you wanted, always deftly slitting somebody's throat with her tongue the way she'd done Max's yesterday.

Could Alice B. have been a happy person? Sarah supposed she must have been reasonably content with the life she'd led. Otherwise, why hadn't she done something else? If she hadn't attached herself to Miffy, no doubt she'd have found another patroness. Some people were born hangers-on. Perhaps that was why Alice B. had to dress up in stagey costumes and search out new dishes to surprise Miffy's guests with and new scandals to titillate them with. Ordinary clothes, ordinary food, and ordinary human courtesy couldn't have disguised the fact that Alice had no genuine life of her own.

Cutting down other people would have been her revenge against them for being real enough to make mistakes and get into situations. Maybe Alice B. had always yearned to become the center of some great drama herself, and never dared to venture into one. One mustn't wish for things, or one would be sure to get them.

Well, this wasn't getting the floor mopped. Even Pete had gone to work finally. She could see him through the window, using the old scythe Alexander had always kept so well sharpened with a whetstone. Pete must be angry about having to mow by hand, from the look on his face. Too bad for him. It was his own fault he'd let the grass grow so high it would have kept binding in the mower. From now on, Sarah decided, she'd funnel all her instructions through old Jed. The less she had to do with Pete Lomax, the better she'd be able to endure having him around.

She still had the apartment over the carriage house to tidy. If Max Bittersohn knew how to make a bed, he'd shown no sign of it since he'd been boarding with her.

They still hadn't got things settled about Barbara, either. Though what was there to settle, actually? Maybe she'd ask him to take her grocery shopping instead. They could swing by Miffy's and leave another bagful of clothes for Aunt Appie in the hope that she'd take the hint and stay longer. Now, if Cousin Lionel could only be palmed off on Miffy, too.

No hope of that. In the first place, Miffy hated children. In the second, she had no land fit for camping; only a quarter acre or so of perfect lawn with a rigidly pruned privet hedge around it and some ornamental shrubs clipped into cones and spheres. Miffy had to show even Mother Nature who was boss.

If it had been Miffy instead of Alice B. who'd got brained with the axe, the killing might have made more sense. Alice B. was vicious and sly, but not violent. Miffy was openly brutal. Anybody who objected to getting jumped on became her sworn enemy.

By now, Miffy had running feuds on with any number of people, many of them year-rounders because she always stayed on so long after the yacht club closed down for the winter and her usual drinking buddies dispersed. Was it in fact possible that Alice B. had been killed in mistake for Miffy? Or was Alice B. so closely identified with her patroness that the killer hadn't cared which one he got? That of course was assuming there'd been anything personal in the killing, which Sarah had no right as yet to assume.

As to that list of stolen items, Sarah didn't know what to make of it. She herself didn't claim any great expertise but she was a trained artist, she'd spent a lot of time at museums and picked up a good deal lately from Max. Moreover, she'd inherited some good things herself and read up on them because she'd had to peddle a few to antique dealers during the early days of her sudden penury.

To her, the list seemed almost too good to be true. Surely Miffy must have owned those particular items or she wouldn't have gone to the expense of insuring them. Miffy couldn't have had much more good stuff, though, or some of it would have been on view and Sarah would have remembered. She'd spent enough time staring at Miffy's walls during her younger days. The burglar must have skimmed off the cream and left the less desirable pieces even though many of them were larger and more showy. This was a connoisseur's crime. How could it fit in with the primitive barbarity of an axe murder?

To believe Alice B. had come downstairs and surprised the robber, then stood patiently waiting in the dining room while he ran around back to the woodpile, fetched the axe, and came back to slaughter her was absurd. To suppose someone intending to steal precious, fragile items like that Bilbao looking glass would encumber himself at the outset with such a heavy, awkward weapon was even sillier.

A knife would have been just as effective and lot easier to manage. Alice B. had slews of fine French steel knives for her gourmet cooking. She'd kept them razor sharp as a cordon-bleu chef ought to, and ready to hand in wooden racks screwed to the kitchen wall. Anybody who knew the house well enough to ferret out its valuables could surely have laid hands on any knife he wanted, or a cleaver if he'd rather hack than stab.

Was it possible two separate crimes had been committed on the same night? Could Alice B. have heard the first burglar leaving, perhaps, and come downstairs only to run into a second who'd had the same idea but a less polished approach?

More likely, the knowledgeable thief had brought a helper. There'd have been considerable fetching and carrying involved even if the items taken weren't large. That Bilbao looking glass alone would have been as much as most people would risk trying to handle at one time. What would be the point in stealing a thing like that if you smashed it getting it out to your car?

They must have had a car, Sarah thought. That wouldn't have presented any great problem. Miffy's house wasn't off in the woods like this one, but situated at the intersection of two roads down in the picturesque part of the old village. Cars were more common than not around there, especially now since the tourists had begun to arrive and there was plenty of hedge to hide one behind.

Suppose the person inside, the one who knew his way around, had been handing loot out the dining room window to a confederate who was taking it to a conveniently parked vehicle. Suppose Alice B. had in fact come downstairs and grappled with the thief, who might even have been a woman no bigger than she. Seeing his partner in trouble, the outside man might have run to get the axe from the woodpile, climbed in the window, and struck Alice B.

That could explain why the dining room silver hadn't been taken. They'd have meant to get the valuable smaller items first, then scoop up the bulky ones on their way out. Once murder had been done, however, they wouldn't have dared do anything but flee. There must have been a certain amount of noise. Maybe Alice had cried out, and they couldn't be sure Miffy would still be deep enough in her drunken stupor not to hear.

Would Alice B. have been reckless enough to attack a burglar single-handed, even if it was somebody she knew? She'd have been drinking, of course, but she wouldn't have been drunk. Perhaps that had been one flaw in what must otherwise have been a well-planned crime. Because Miffy never went to bed sober if she could help it, everybody tended to take it for granted Alice B. didn't, either.

In fact, however, Alice B. had been clever about pretending to keep up with the rest of the crowd while secretly watering her drinks with innumerable ice cubes so that she'd be able to keep her wits together and not miss anything. Miffy's brand of hospitality being what it was, most of her guests had probably gone home fairly well anaesthetized last night, but Alice B. ought to have remained sober enough. Early on, she'd been occupied with her clam puffs. After the cocktail party broke up, some of the crowd would surely have stayed for supper. That meant she'd have been doing her thing in the kitchen, flipping crepes or whipping up two perfect omelets at a time with a frying pan in each hand while the rest sat around the big kitchen table swilling wine and cheering her on.

She wouldn't have drunk the wine herself. Putting on a show for company would have been intoxication enough for Alice B. When the guests at last cleared off, there'd have been a mess to clean up and Miffy to put to bed because by then the hostess would have been out on her feet. By the time Alice B. got a chance to rest, she'd hardly have required a nightcap to put her to sleep.

Alice B. couldn't have been any youngster, after all. She must have been at least Appie Kelling's age, and Sarah herself had baked the cake for Appie's sixtieth birthday party ages ago, when Uncle Samuel was still able to be up and about. It was surprising Alice B. had been able to manage as well as she had, especially with tasks like getting Miffy undressed and decently tucked into bed.

Aunt Appie would have that honor tonight, no doubt. Sarah folded a nightgown her aunt had left thrown over the foot of the guest room bed and laid it back in the suitcase Appie hadn't bothered to finish unpacking. Just as well she hadn't. Now it would be easy to close the case and cart it over to Miffy's.

As she straightened up, Sarah glanced out the window to see how Pete was getting on with the mowing. Was that a dog sneaking up through the tall grass behind him? No, a dog wouldn't be wearing a green and purple striped rugby shirt. It had to be one of Lionel's brats. What was he doing up here? If Pete — good God!

"Hey!"

That was the boy shouting. Alive, thank heaven. He'd leaped straight into the air as Pete whirled around and swung the scythe blade viciously through the weeds where he'd been lurking.

"Pete!" Sarah screamed out the window. "You could have killed that boy."

"Yeah? Well — " the hired man was shaken, Sarah could see that. Still he couldn't help twisting his lips in a self-satisfied smirk. "I got fast reflexes."

"Then you'd better slow them down. Stop crying, Woody. I'm coming."

It was typical of Lionel and Vare that they'd named their first three sons Jesse, Woodson, and James. The fourth and no doubt last now that Vare had switched her sexual proclivities, was Frank, of course.

Max was just finishing a phone call when Sarah got downstairs. "Sorry I couldn't cut that short," he apologized. "I was talking to a guy at the Sûreté. Don't look at me like that. I charged it to my business account. What's all the hullabaloo out back?"

"Pete Lomax just tried to chop one of

Lionel's boys in two with the scythe."

"Any particular reason?"

"Woody was playing the fool, sneaking up through the grass. He startled Pete, and Pete swung on him. He claims he has fast reflexes. I've got to go out there."

"I'll go with you," said Max. "I know all about Pete's fast reflexes. Remind me to show you his footprint in spike marks on my thigh, if our acquaintance ever progresses that far."

When they got out back, Woody was still blubbering from the shock. Pete was unconcernedly cutting grass. Sarah blew up.

"Pete, if you can't handle tools in a responsible manner, you'd better leave them alone."

"You told me to cut the grass."

"I told you three weeks ago. If you'd done it then, this would never have happened. You'll either learn to take orders or find somewhere else to work. As for you, Woody, what were you doing up here in the first place? I told you to stay away from the main house, didn't I? Why aren't you down at the camp where you belong?"

"I want to make a phone call," he growled.

"Then walk down to the pay phone in the village."

"Why the hell should I?"

"Because you're not going to use mine, that's why. Now get out of here and don't come back. You've caused enough trouble and I shan't stand for any more."

"Boy, some summer this is going to be."

Kicking a stone in front of him, the boy slumped off down the drive. Sarah turned to Max.

"I'm going to clean the carriage house. You may as well come with me and help. The way things are shaping up around here, don't be surprised if you wind up having to do your own housework."

That was mostly for Pete's benefit, since Max would have come anyway. And why should Sarah feel self-conscious about what Pete Lomax was no doubt thinking about her and her handsome tenant? Furious with herself, Sarah strode down over the hill to the carriage house.

CHAPTER 8

"I suppose I was rather awful to poor Woody."

Sarah was fussing around trying to pretend Max's dresser needed tidying though he'd barely spent enough time in the room to clutter it up and was reasonably neat in his habits anyway.

"The trouble with Lionel's tribe is that if you try to treat them like human beings, they turn around and stamp all over you. Not that they get it from anybody strange."

"That mother of theirs must be pretty damn strange, walking out on four young kids to go and shack up with another woman."

Max came over and put his hands on either side of Sarah's waist. "I've been wondering, Sarah. How do you feel about kids?"

"Kids in general or kids in particular?"

"Our kids, damn it."

Sarah leaned her head back against his chest. "You know something, Max? You're just an old-fashioned paterfamilias."

"Who the hell said I wasn't? They wouldn't be Jewish, you know."

"Why wouldn't they?"

"Because the religion descends through the mother."

"Does that mean they could never play in the Maccabean Chess Tournament?"

"These things have to be faced, my love."

"That's discriminatory and rotten!" Sarah cried. "I didn't know Jews were such snobs."

"You thought your crowd had a monopoly on snobbery?"

"Don't call them my crowd. You wouldn't identify me with Fren Larrington and Miffy Tergoyne, I should hope?"

"It's what you were born into, Sarah. Like it or lump it, you'll never quite be able to shake them."

"What are you trying to say, that engraven on my heart are a bean and a cod?"

"And on mine a schmalz herring." Max rubbed his cheek against her soft, fine hair. "How about it, *fischele?* Do we start our own aquarium?"

"Miz Kelling! Miz Kelling!"

Old Jed Lomax was running up the drive, bellowing his lungs out. Sarah sighed.

"Max, do you have the feeling we're hopelessly outnumbered?"

She ran to the window and stuck her head out. "I'm down here, Mr. Lomax, in the carriage house. What's the matter?"

"I got to use the phone, quick. Them kids set fire to the boathouse."

"Oh Lord, what next? I'll call."

She grabbed Max's telephone. "Operator? Get me the Ireson's Fire Department quickly, please. It's an emergency. Max, you'd better go down there with Mr. Lomax and see how bad it is. I could slaughter Cousin — hello? Hello, this is Mrs. Kelling over on Wood Lane. My cousin's children have set fire to our boathouse. Could you come right away, please, before it spreads to the trees?"

If it hadn't already. Sarah thought she could smell smoke. "Yes, the big place on the hill. Mr. Lomax will be at the end of the drive to show you where to go."

"Mr. Lomax," she shouted down, "I said you'd be down by the road to show them the path."

"Then I better get goin'. Thanks, Miz Kelling."

"Don't thank *me*," she burbled semihys-

111

terically, but nobody was left to hear her. Max and old Jed were already on their way. Pete had no doubt heard his uncle shouting and was off to the fire, also. Sarah hoped he'd left the scythe behind him.

But he might at least have taken a broom and a bucket. She'd remembered Alexander's private fire department. Her late husband had been a great one for preparedness. Both at the main house and down here, he'd gathered together a collection of old brooms, burlap sacks, and galvanized pails in case of such an emergency as this. Sarah had teased him about them, but Alexander had taken his equipment seriously.

"Big fires start from little ones, Sarah. Isolated as we are out here, we can't afford to take risks. Some day we may be glad we have these things handy."

For him, that day had never come. It was the least his widow could do to put them to use now. Why hadn't Mr. Lomax remembered? Probably he had, and realized they'd be futile.

Nevertheless, Sarah grabbed up the brooms and buckets, flung the sacks over her shoulders, and struggled down over the hill with her clattering load. She'd tramped these woods often enough to know every shortcut, so she got to the fire almost as soon as Max, who'd run down the drive and come in by the path.

Cousin Lionel was, she saw, handling the crisis as one might expect: urging his sons to help him strike the tent and rescue their camping equipment, not raising a hand to save the boathouse or keep the fire in the grass from spreading to the woods. She brushed past him and began handing out sacks and brooms.

"Jesse, take this bucket and fill it with water. Boys, wet these sacks and start beating out the fire over there around the edges. We've got to keep it away from the trees. Lionel, give Max the keys to your van. It's blocking the path so the fire engines can't get through."

"No!" shouted her cousin. "I need the van to save the tent."

"If that gas tank explodes, you won't save anything, including yourself," Max told him. "The keys, Lionel."

Lionel took one look at the set of Max's jaw and handed over the keys. Max leaped into the high driver's seat, jockeyed the vehicle away from the creeping flames, and bumped off through the as yet unharmed trees.

Pete appeared about that time, apparently

set to loll back and enjoy the show. Sarah handed him a broom and a bucket and told him to get busy.

"Help me with the tent first," Lionel screamed.

Pete paid no attention to him. Neither did any of his sons. They were much more interested in beating at the flames and daring each other to jump on sparks in their bare feet. Then the pumper lurched into the clearing, Jed Lomax clinging to the back along with a couple of other auxiliary firemen. Their first move was to snatch up Cousin Lionel's brand-new gasoline stove and lantern, and pitch them down on the rocks. Their next was to ignore his bellows of rage and get busy hooking up their hoses to pump water from the ocean.

"Lucky tide's on the make," grunted one of them. "Woods are dry for the time of year. Quit blethering about that tent, Mister. It's fire-retardant, or ought to be. If not, we'd have to confiscate it anyway."

Lionel subsided into wrathful mutters and baleful glares as he continued to fuss over the incredible amount of gear he'd thought necessary for roughing it on his cousin's estate. A second engine with yet more firemen arrived and obliged him by soaking down everything including the sleeping bags, the spare clothing, and Cousin Lionel himself. They tried to make him believe they hadn't done it on purpose.

With that big a crew, the fire was soon out, although the firemen hung around spraying the clearing for a while and giving Cousin Lionel's gear another bath or two in the process. They hadn't been able to save the boathouse. That had already been almost gone by the time they'd got here.

"Any idea how the fire started, Mrs. Kelling?" the fire chief asked her.

"You'd better ask my cousin," she replied, glaring at the hapless Lionel. "He invited himself to camp here. I'd given him strict warning about keeping his children out of mischief, but apparently it didn't sink in."

"We didn't set it," yelled Jesse.

"We couldn't," squeaked little Frank. "Lionel put all the matches in a waterproof match safe and now he can't get the top off."

"Oh yeah?" said the chief. "Let's see this match safe."

Sullenly, Lionel fished through his sodden heap of gear and managed to excavate the matchbox. The chief studied it for a second, flicked something with his thumbnail, and the top slid open.

"Lionel's a jerk," James observed.

"Why don't you belt that kid?" suggested one of the firemen.

"I do not approve of using violence against children," Lionel replied through gritted teeth. "As you see, no matches are missing. I packed them in tightly so that they could not rattle around and ignite by accident."

"You sure did. The way you've got 'em crammed in, you'd probably set fire to the whole boxful if you tried to pry one out. And you don't have any other matches but these? No cigarette lighter?"

"I don't smoke."

"What about your sons? Come on, kids. Which of you had the matches?"

They all poked each other and snickered, but nobody confessed.

"Won't squeal on each other, eh?" said the chief.

"That's a change," Sarah remarked. "Usually they're blaming each other for everything. Boys, this is no time to be noble. You needn't think keeping quiet is going to let Lionel off the hook. No matter who set the fire, your father's going to pay up if it gets me into trouble with the bank."

That struck the children as hilarious, but still no confession was forthcoming. Jesse peeled off his shorts and jersey, and hurled them at the fire chief's feet.

"Search me," he commanded.

Since neither the shorts nor the jersey had any pockets and Jesse wasn't wearing anything underneath, his point was conclusive. In a moment his two younger brothers were also yelling, "Search me," and capering around in their mosquito-bitten pelts.

"Shut up and put your clothes on," Sarah yelled. "What about Woody? Did he have any matches?"

"He didn't have no more on than these kids here," Pete Lomax put in, as if he felt he might owe Woody a favor after having almost dismembered him. "At least not when I seen him up at the main house," he amended lest anybody think him too forthcoming.

"Was that the one I seen goin' down the drive?" his uncle asked. "Skinny runt in his bare feet like these here? Wearin' one o' them striped tops like the bathin' suit my Uncle Arch used to sport around in long about 1910, except Uncle Arch's suit had longer pants to it?"

"That must have been Woody," said

Sarah. "Where did he go, Mr. Lomax?"

"Dunno's I could say. He didn't come back this way, nohow. Went straight on past me an' turned up the road toward the village. He didn't look none too happy, but he wasn't runnin' nor nothin'."

"How come Woody was going to the village?" Jesse demanded. "He told me he was going up to use Sarah's phone. He wanted to call his bookie."

"Woody has a turn for finance," Lionel explained. "He is conducting experiments involving various forms of speculation."

"He's got a tip on the fifth at Suffolk Downs," Jesse interpreted. "He's trying to raise enough money to run away to Bora Bora while he's still eligible for a kid's rate on the plane fare."

"Sounds reasonable," Max Bittersohn remarked.

"Yes, well, I'm afraid I stifled his initiative," Sarah said. "I told him he'd have to go down to the pay station in the village. If I'd known the call was for a worthy cause, I might have reconsidered. How long ago did he leave here, and did he go into the boathouse alone before he went?"

"We all explored the interior together," Lionel told her.

"Yeah, Lionel showed us where the can was," James giggled. "What do we do now, Lionel? Head for the bushes?"

"I'd suggest you head straight back to Cambridge," was Sarah's solution. "You'll never get those sleeping bags dry enough to use tonight and I'm certainly not going to ask you up to the house after this even if I had enough bedding, which I don't. When I said you wouldn't be allowed to stay here if you caused any trouble, I meant it."

Little Frank snorted. "Jeez, what a dope. She still thinks we torched the joint."

"If you didn't, who did? There was no electrical wiring in the boathouse. I can't think what else could have gone wrong enough to start a fire. Can you, Mr. Lomax?"

"What about the plumbing?" the fire chief interrupted. "How did that work, Mrs. Kelling?"

"Water had to be pumped up by hand from an underground well. It was an old system and I'm sure it was ruined by the fire. Honestly, Lionel, I'd like to strangle you!"

"Yay," shouted Jesse. "You heard her, everybody. Now we can murder Lionel and lay the blame on Sarah."

"That's right, lads," said their father with a painful attempt at a smile. "Get those nasty old aggressions out of your systems before they have a chance to build up and cause trouble."

"I'm not getting rid of mine until I've heard what the insurance people have to say," Sarah told him.

"My dear Sarah, if you can explain to me how I or any of my sons managed to start that fire when we had nothing to light it with, I shall be entirely amenable to paying whatever damages have been incurred."

That was a facer. Lionel must be alarmingly confident of his position or he'd never make such a statement in front of witnesses. Kellings were not apt to go out on limbs when questions of cash disbursement were being discussed, and Lionel was considered a touch on the near side, even for a Kelling.

But if the boys hadn't started the fire, who had? Sarah couldn't believe it had been set off by sunlight focusing through a broken bottle or any such fluke as that, because the day had been overcast ever since Aunt Appie had drizzled that lukewarm tea down her neck. Nor could it have been spontaneous combustion because there'd been nothing in the boathouse to combust.

Alexander had always been careful about keeping oily rags or inflammable substances around, and so had Mr. Lomax.

"Mr. Lomax," she asked, "when did you last check the boathouse? Before this morning, I mean."

"On my reg'lar rounds yesterday," he told her promptly enough. "In the mornin' when I come to make sure things was ready for you, 'cause I knew you'd be comin' along."

"If you knew we were coming, why didn't you have the electricity turned on?"

That was Max asking. Sarah herself wouldn't have embarrassed the caretaker by raising the question in front of his buddies from the fire department. Old Jed was not unnaturally resentful.

"What do you mean, why didn't I? O' course I turned it on, same as I always do."

"Then somebody else must have turned it off again because the lights weren't working when we got here. Remember, Sarah?"

Sarah had to nod. She distinctly recalled flicking the switches in vain when Max had wanted to examine the elegant relic they'd so mysteriously found in the front entryway. That was why Mr. Lomax had found them out on the front lawn with Jofferty a little while later. They'd been so intrigued by the Bilbao looking glass then that she hadn't thought to mention the oversight. She and Max had wound up later on throwing the main switch themselves.

It hadn't been like Mr. Lomax to forget. It was even more unlike him to be so positive now, unless he knew for an absolute dead certainty that he'd done the job he was supposed to do. So Lomax must have turned on the electricity when he claimed he had and somebody else had come along shortly afterward and turned it off again. Whatever for?

The obvious culprit was his nephew Pete, but why should Pete have pulled a silly trick like that? Of course if Sarah had happened to come and catch him at it, he could have pretended to be changing a blown fuse or something. As to getting access to the fuse box, the pair of them might have been in and out of the house two or three times that morning, making sure the water was running properly and whatnot. They wouldn't have locked up until they were ready to leave.

But what would Pete have gained by turning off the lights? He might have done it just to be nasty, she supposed, or to make it look as if his uncle was getting beyond the job and a younger man such as himself ought be hired instead. Or he might not have wanted Sarah to come into that dark entryway and switch on the lights in time to catch him hanging a Bilbao looking glass he'd just swiped from Miffy Tergoyne's.

It was not wholly beyond the realm of possibility that somebody had sneaked in and stolen the glass right after Miffy and Alice B. had taken inventory, since they'd no doubt gone straight to the kitchen afterward for a late breakfast and an early pick-me-up. But why bring the thing here, knowing Sarah would be along soon?

Why not think of something more sensible, like calling in the electrician to check the wiring? Maybe there was a loose connection in the main switch or something. Anyway, whatever had happened to the lights yesterday at the main house couldn't have any thing to do with the fire down here today. Could it? Sarah wished she could believe the boys were lying about not having any matches, but she had a nasty feeling they weren't.

"I don't suppose we have an arson squad at Ireson Town," she said to the fire chief, "but could you possibly call in someone from somewhere? I hate to be more of a pest than I've been to you already, but the insurance company will be on my back about this. So will the bank people. I must have some kind of answer for them."

"Wasn't any gasoline or oil stored here?" he asked her. "For a boat, I mean?"

"The family hadn't owned a boat since long before I was married. To the best of my knowledge, there was nothing here that could have been considered burnable except the boathouse itself. If Mr. Lomax says he inspected the place yesterday morning, you can be absolutely sure he did. That means there wouldn't have been any unauthorized person camping here, either. We have been bothered with them sometimes in the past; that's why Mr. Lomax is always so particular about checking around down here. Furthermore, he and his nephew have both been spending a lot of extra time here lately because we've had so many projects going. I've been coming out most days myself, although I just moved in officially, as you might say, yesterday. Oh, and this is my tenant, Mr. Bittersohn."

"Isaac Bittersohn's boy from Saugus," Mr. Lomax amplified.

"Hell, yes, I heard you were in town," said the chief. "How's your father? Say, did anybody ever tell you about the time we got Isaac to put a new roof on the fire station?"

The firemen clustered around, off on a long-winded saga. Max was smiling and nodding and having his hand shaken and his back slapped and being invited to drop over and meet the firehouse dog whom they'd named Isaac as a gesture of highest esteem. Sarah was out of it again. While the men chatted and laughed, she poked among the warm, wet ashes of the boathouse, and wondered.

CHAPTER 9

"At least that ill wind blew some good."

Sarah and Max were having a picnic lunch by themselves out by the cliff, where they could look down at the water and forget the devastation below the hill. Cousin Lionel had loaded his wet camping gear into the van, rounded up his tribe, and gone off to run the sleeping bags through the dryer at the village laundromat, as Sarah was so inconsiderate as not to own one and the sun wouldn't oblige by coming out and doing the job for nothing.

No doubt he'd stop at Miffy's on his way. He'd stand a fat chance of getting to use any dryer of hers. He might get lunch for himself and the boys, though, and he'd surely give his mother an earful about the unkind reception they'd received from Sarah.

She should worry. Maybe Aunt Appie

would be so hurt by Sarah's coldness that she'd never come back, either. With any luck, one might get one's self ostracized by the entire yacht club set. It was a beautiful thought. Sarah scowled at a sea gull that was loudly demanding a share of her sandwich.

"Shut up and go catch a fish. I'm sick of moochers. Max, do you think I'm getting hardhearted?"

"Me you're asking?" He pushed up her sleeve and planted a somewhat mustardy kiss in the crook of her elbow. "You're in a period of transition, that's what."

"Where did you pick up that one? Oh, I know. The psychiatrist whose patient pinched his Toulouse-Lautrec."

"Smart kid. I like this place."

"So do I. I hope we get to keep it."

"If you had to choose between this and the Boston house, which would you pick?"

"Need you ask? I've been phased out of Tulip Street. Theonia and Brooks and Mariposa and Charles are managing far better than I ever did. Right now I don't even have a room there."

She'd turned over her own second-floor suite to Theonia and Brooks, and rented Theonia's old room on the third floor for the summer to a scholar from Mount Holyoke who was in town doing research on a biography of Phyllis Wheatley. Professor Ormsby was gone and an executive from some computer company who'd just been transferred was living in his place while house-hunting. Even Max's basement lair had been taken over by an actor friend of Charles's who was starring in a show at the Wilbur, though nobody knew for how long. There'd have to be a major turnover in the fall, but Sarah didn't have to think about that now. Maybe she'd never have to bother herself at all.

"I wonder what it would be like living here in the winter?" she said dreamily.

"Cold as hell," Max grunted.

"Of course the big house would be impossible, but if we insulated the carriage house and put in a couple of wood stoves and a kitchen — "

"Now you're talking, *kätzele*." Max took her hand and hauled her to her feet. "Come on, let's go buy a stove."

"Why don't we just walk along the beach and gather driftwood? Then we can curl up in front of the fireplace later and give the project some serious thought."

"You're not going to that yacht club thing?"

"What yacht club thing? Oh, you mean Fren Larrington. Certainly not, why should I? I barely know Fren, for goodness' sake. He never paid the slightest bit of attention to me while Alexander was alive. None of them did, except Bradley Rovedock sometimes, when he happened to be around. They used to treat me like part of the furniture. I don't know why they're bothering me now. I suppose they think they're comforting me in my bereavement, but I wish they wouldn't."

Sarah relented and threw the last bit of crust to the still importunate gull. "Besides, that wasn't an invitation. It was an order Fren had no earthly right to give. I fail to see why I should even dignify it by a refusal. Anyway, with this ghastly business about Alice B., I don't expect anybody will feel like partying tonight. Fren mustn't have heard, or else the news hadn't had time to sink in. He's pretty dense about everything but sailing."

"Since you're free, then, how'd you like to come and meet my Uncle Jake? He was asking me about you last night. He's staying with Miriam and Ira for a few days."

"I'd adore to, Max. I wish I could ask them all here instead, but things are in such a turmoil there's no telling what they'd be letting themselves in for if they came. What time would Miriam expect us?"

"When would you like to go? They generally eat about half-past six so that Mike can get off to his night classes. Is that too early for you?"

"No, but we can't go barging in at dinnertime without an invitation."

"Why not?"

Because it wasn't the done thing; except that among the Bittersohn clan it evidently was. One could always bring something, she supposed. Like Aunt Appie. Sarah began to laugh.

"I know. I'll throw together a nice tuna casserole."

Max laughed, too. "What happened to the other one?"

"I was so furious last night that I served it. Nobody ate much — if you'd been around you'd have known why — so I set the rest out for the animals. Maybe it was the raccoons who burned down the boathouse in revenge for their tummyaches. Max, I hate to say this but I have an awful feeling Lionel's monsters were telling the truth."

"I don't like it any more than you do,

but I'm afraid you're right," he agreed. "I wonder if the arson squad will be able to turn up anything."

"I hope so. It would be awful, never knowing. Remember that man with the jug of paint thinner who tried to burn down the house in Boston?"

"How could I ever forget? That was the first time you ever bothered to call me up."

"And I've been bothering you ever since."

"Damn right you have." He pulled her over to him.

Blam! The noise of a cannon shot reverberated from the cliffside.

"My God!" Bittersohn pushed Sarah face down into the grass and flung himself on top of her. "We're under bombardment."

To his amazement, she was laughing. "Thus conscience doth make cowards of us all. That's the starting cannon for a sailboat race, you idiot. We just happened to hear it more clearly than usual because it's right below us. They must be practicing for the early regatta. I thought I heard another signal a while back, but one gets so used to them out here, one doesn't pay attention. Bradley Rovedock's the starter, I shouldn't wonder. He never competes because *Perdita* can outsail any other boat in the club. They ought to be sailing past here any moment now."

"Great," said Bittersohn in disgust. "With their spyglasses glued to their eyeballs so they can see what we're up to, no doubt. Let's go over to the station and watch Ira pump gas."

"Whatever turns you on, as our dear Miss LaValliere would say. I personally don't see why we shouldn't continue to sit here in a sedate and decorous manner, and enjoy the spectacle."

"You would have to drag in the sedate and decorous manner."

"One of us has to observe the proprieties. Look, there's the first sail coming out of the cove now. Fren Larrington, I'll bet. He's crowding it on for all she's worth. Watch, he's going to pick up that little ruffle of wind you can see on the water out there and stand away from the cliff. A novice would stay close to land thinking to shorten the course, and get hung up in irons, like as not."

"I didn't realize sailing was such a brutal sport."

"Aren't you the funny one? That just means having the wind dead ahead of you so that you can't move until you fall off and come about. Fall off doesn't mean fall off the boat, of course. It's all very technical. Alexander used to explain this stuff to me. We'd be standing here and — Max darling, I am sorry. I honestly don't mean to keep running on about the past. It's just like — oh, your talking about your Uncle Jake. Someone you've known all your life."

"I was never married to Uncle Jake."

"Max, can't you understand it wasn't a bit like you and me? Good heavens, there's Miffy Tergoyne's boat. The eighteen-foot gaff-rigged sloop with the red stripe around the hull coming up behind Biff Beaxitt. Biff's too close-hauled as usual. He'll jibe if he doesn't — see there, he just did. Serves him right. I wish I could see who's sailing Miffy's boat."

Rather incredibly, Max took a tiny collapsible telescope out of his pocket. "Give a look."

"My stars, you do come equipped, don't you?"

She leaned against him regardless of whoever might be watching from below, and looked up into his face. "I suppose Barbara used to tell you that."

"Damn it, Sarah, that was a wholly —

okay, I get your point. Who's in Miffy's boat?"

"I do believe that's Miffy herself at the tiller, and Lionel handling the sheets. Aunt Appie must be riding herd on the boys. Wouldn't you know?"

"Some people have a natural taste for martyrdom," said Max. "Your cousin Lionel doesn't appear to be one of them, though. To my untutored eye, he and Miss Tergoyne don't seem to be doing too badly."

The red sloop, which had been far behind, was beginning to work its way up through the scattering of bright sails and shining hulls.

"They're doing very well," Sarah agreed. "Here, want a squint?"

She handed him back his spyglass. "Miffy's a surprisingly good sailor, and Lionel's first-rate. He even crews for Bradley at Newport."

"Who takes care of the kids that day?"

"It's hardly a one-day affair. I expect Vare's always been stuck with them. Maybe that's why she decided she's through with men. Look, they're pulling ahead. Fren will be livid."

"Poor loser, is he?"

"The absolute worst. He'll be smashing everything in sight at the club tonight, I shouldn't wonder. The steward keeps a special set of plastic dishes for when Fren Larrington gets skunked in a race. I'm glad we're not going to be there. Which brings us to the question of what I should take to Miriam. Do you suppose she'd care for some fresh lettuce out of the garden?"

Max said lettuce would be great, so they strolled down to the garden, fought off the gulls, and gathered a fine assortment of early vegetables. Sarah took the stuff back to the house to be washed and crisped in cold water until they were ready to leave; then they went along to find out what progress, if any, was being made among the ruins. They discovered Jed Lomax and his nephew dismantling what little was left of the boathouse and throwing the charred remains into the caretaker's truck.

"You mustn't do that," Sarah cried. "The arson squad is supposed to come and find out how the fire started."

"They already been," Mr. Lomax told her. "Brought the insurance adjustor with 'em. Leastways he come about the same time. Pawed around through the ashes for a while and couldn't find nothin', so they went away again. Pete an' me decided we'd better get rid o' this mess here. Leave it layin' an' you'd have a pack o' young hoodlums up here tonight tryin' to burn what's left of it. Don't worry, Miz Kelling. We're keepin' our eyes peeled. If we turn up anythin', we'll let you know."

"What's your personal opinion, Jed?" asked Max.

"Them damn brats o' Mr. Lionel's, if Miz Kelling don't mind me sayin' so. I dunno what else it could o' been, 'less somebody snuck up in a rowboat an' took a blowtorch to the shingles."

"Hardly seems likely, but you never know."

Max sauntered down to the water's edge. Sarah followed him. The tide had turned by now, and the stone foundation was bared. They could see where somebody had hacked a date into the rocks. That must have been the year the boathouse was built: 1887. Just short of a century.

One might have visions of dashing young men in thick white flannels and brightly ribboned straw boaters helping muslined young ladies with veils and parasols in and out of well-cushioned punts, if one hadn't known the Kellings as Sarah did. In fact, the men would have been wearing whatever came handy and the women fending for themselves in draggled cotton skirts and muddy canvas shoes.

There wouldn't have been any cushions. They'd all have been sunburned and insect-plagued and firm in their conviction that they were setting a good example to the rest of the world. Perhaps the boathouse hadn't meant as much to the world at large as the Kellings might have thought it did, but its passing marked the end of an era nevertheless. Sarah shivered, wondering if this could be an omen of bigger losses to come.

CHAPTER 10

"So I said to the judge, 'Your honor, what's to object? The defendant knows he's committing perjury, your honor knows it, learned counsel for the defense knows it, the jury knows it. Why should I *verdreh my kop* objecting? Let him talk and lose his own case for me.' "

Uncle Jake reminded Sarah a lot of her own beloved Uncle Jem, except that his figure was trimmer, his accent different, and his anecdotes funnier. She was having a marvelous time. Her offering of fresh greens had made a big hit since the Rivkins had no space or inclination for a vegetable garden. Miriam had forthwith tossed up a tremendous salad, every leaf of which had got eaten along with a good many other things. Sarah felt as if she'd swallowed a sofa pillow. No matter, she'd work it off tomorrow doing some of the work that hadn't got done today.

Mike had excused himself and gone off to Boston while they were dawdling over fruit and tea, but it wasn't until he arrived home again that anybody realized how long they'd sat. Sarah pulled herself together and stood up.

"I'm sorry. I've been enjoying myself so much I had no idea how late it is. Max, do let's leave so these poor people can go to bed. I'm sure Ira has to be at work early tomorrow."

"Darn right he does." Ira got up, too. He was a good-looking man with a ready smile and a small spare tire around his waist, which was appropriate to his profession and a natural consequence of Miriam's superb cooking. He'd been talking in an easy, well-informed way about antique cars, the government's Mideast policy — not that he really believed it had one — and a surprising range of other topics.

Miriam was as well-up on them all as he, and not always in agreement with her husband's views. She looked a lot like Max and must be quite stunning when she was dressed up. Tonight she had on a simple denim skirt and a pullover she'd finished knitting for Mike just as he'd outgrown it and wasn't about to let go to waste.

No Kelling would have faulted that sort of logic. Sarah felt quite at home with the Rivkins, and far better entertained than she would have been with many of her own clan.

"Enjoy yourself?" Max asked when they'd at last got themselves out to his car and headed back to the other end of town.

"Tremendously. I do like them all so much. They seem to like each other, too. Don't they ever fight?"

"Wait till you meet my mother. If you're tired, you could put your head on my shoulder," he added helpfully.

Sarah thought that was a splendid idea, even though it induced Max to put his arm around her and she knew people weren't supposed to drive one-handed. Somehow that didn't bother her as much as it should have. She was in a mood of dreamy contentment, until they topped the drive to find the house ablaze with lights and two cars parked out in front.

"My God, what now?"

Sarah scrambled out of the low seat and ran into the house, Max at her heels telling her in frantic tones to keep calm. They were met by Aunt Appie in a dreadful state.

"Oh, Sarah, thank heaven you're back! We were beside ourselves."

"Why? What's happened?"

"You never showed up at the club!"

"Aunt Appie, you don't mean to tell me you've worked yourself into a tizzy on my account? I never go to the club, if I can help it. I'm not even a member. You ought to know that."

"But Fren Larrington distinctly told me he'd invited you as his guest."

"Fren barged in here this morning, ordered me to get there under my own steam, then left without giving me a chance to tell him I had no transportation and didn't want to go anyway because I had better things to do. Maybe you call that an invitation. I don't."

"Sarah dear, Fren took it for granted — "

"What right has Fren Larrington to take me for granted? He's never looked crosswise at me before and I hope he never does again. Anyway, I naturally assumed neither he nor anybody else would feel like partying once the news about Alice B. got around."

"But that was the whole point, dear. We were trying to cheer Miffy up."

"That was kind of you," Sarah told her aunt wearily, "but what did it have to do with me? Don't you recall that right after you got here yesterday I told you to go ahead and make any plans you wanted with your friends, but to leave me out of them because I have too many projects of my own going?"

"Darling, you might at least have told me."

"I just got through reminding you that I did tell you. Furthermore, what with Lionel's tribe burning down my boathouse about five minutes after they got here this morning, this has been an exceptionally distracting day for me."

Sarah was sorry she'd said that, but she needn't have been. It was the sort of thing her aunt simply didn't hear.

"Fren was dreadfully disappointed."

"He'll get over it. I'm sorry you put your friends through this for nothing. If you think I owe an apology, please consider it given and thank you for being concerned enough to come. Can I offer anybody a cup of coffee before you leave?"

"You might at least tell us where you've been."

Sarah was startled. She'd realized there were other people in the room, but she'd been too furious with her aunt to notice who they were. That high-pitched whine could only be Pussy Beaxitt's. Pussy wasn't losing any time snatching up Alice B.'s fallen torch as official newsmonger for the crowd. She wouldn't depart without an answer, so Sarah might as well come across.

"Considering the state I appear to have gotten you all into, I wish I had something exciting to tell. In fact, however, Max and I have been spending a very pleasant evening with his people over at the other end of town."

"His people? You mean that Rivkin who runs the gas station?"

Pussy made her incredulous derision as offensive as possible. Her husband Biff emitted a snort of either laughter or outrage, not that it mattered which.

Bradley Rovedock, who'd been hanging back in the shadows no doubt wishing he hadn't got roped into this, stepped forward.

"I'm glad to see you making new friends, Sarah, but I'm selfish enough to hope you won't forget the old ones. My own purpose for coming along on this rather impertinent late visit tonight was to see whether I could lure you out tomorrow for a day cruise aboard *Perdita*. Mr. Bittersohn too, of course, if he'd care to come. Appie's going to be busy with Miffy, she tells me, but Lassie and Don Larrington have said they'll join us. I thought we might run over to Little Nibble and pay a short call on the Ganlors."

"Thanks," said Max, "but I have to be out of town. Why don't you go, Sarah? The change might do you good."

If she'd thought Max was tactfully effacing himself, Sarah would have refused like a shot. He'd told her on the way to Miriam's, though, that he had to catch the early shuttle to New York in quest of a Titian stolen from the Wilkins Museum. There was no telling when he'd be back, so she might as well accept Bradley's invitation. It was the least she could do after the bother he'd been put to on her behalf.

Besides, a day sail to Little Nibble had always been one of Sarah's most particular summertime treats. She adored the Ganlors, who were still holding aloft the banner of transcendentalism well over a century after the Fruitlands colony had given it up. She even enjoyed listening to them quote Bronson Alcott as if they actually understood what he'd been driving at; though her own thoughts tended to be with the original counterparts of Marmee, Meg, Jo, Beth, and Amy, out slopping the hogs and digging potatoes while Papa composed his profundities.

Sarah knew what the day would be like because she'd done it so many times before. Bradley's housekeeper would have packed a huge wicker hamper full of cold chicken, salad, ineffable little pastries, with chilled white wine to go with the lunch and hot drinks in thermos bottles for the sail home when the sun began to sink and the wind to rise. There would be no endless round of cocktails. On Little Nibble there'd be nothing but herb tea or lemonade because the Ganlors went in for plain living and high thinking on a scale not to be believed by the uninitiated.

"Thank you, Bradley," she said. "I'd love to come. What time shall I be ready?"

They settled on nine o'clock, then the lot of them cleared out, mercifully taking Aunt Appie and the photograph album with them. Appie thought she'd show the album to Miffy tomorrow, to take her mind off Alice B.'s upcoming funeral.

"That's assuming Miffy ever comes out of the stupor she drank herself into tonight," said Biff Beaxitt.

"You're a fine one to talk," snapped his

wife. "Here, give me those car keys. You're in no fit state to drive, yourself."

After the cars had pulled away, Max said to Sarah, "I think I'll take a look around, if you don't mind. I don't want to scare you, but after what Lomax told us about the light switches, it looks to me as if somebody may have a key to this place. You'd better leave some of these lights on downstairs, just in case. I could sleep over, if you like," he added helpfully.

"Do you think for one second Pussy Beaxitt isn't going to come sneaking back after she's got Biff stashed away, to find out what we're up to?" Sarah asked him. "Don't worry about me. I expect there's a spy behind every shrub in the back yard waiting to see whether you go back to the carriage house or not. I couldn't be better protected in the Franklin Park Zoo."

"Yeah, well, they get plenty of trouble around Franklin Park, too," Max grunted.

Sarah gave him a kiss on the nose. "Go ahead and do your prowl if it will make you feel better. I'm going to fix you a thermos of coffee and something to eat before you leave tomorrow morning. I don't want you catching that plane on an empty stomach and getting airsick."

"I never get airsick."

"There's always a first time. I do hate to think of your having to start out so early. We should have left Miriam's ages ago, but I was having such fun. And then Aunt Appie had to go and spoil it all. I might have known she'd go into a tizzy when I didn't show up at that stupid dinner."

"But you didn't expect her to be at the club either," Max reminded her. "Cheer up, kid. Now they know what kind of company you're keeping, they'll drop you like a hot potato."

"Don't you believe it. They'll all be hounding me to use my influence with Ira to get them free tune-ups. Well, not all of them, I don't suppose. Aunt Appie wouldn't, but then she doesn't drive. Lionel would, you can bet. I wonder who got stuck with him tonight."

"I fully expect to find him and the wolf pack tucked up in your bed."

"If you do, we'll call the police. Go see, for goodness' sake, then get on to bed yourself."

The rooms proved empty of anything but a few mosquitos that Max gallantly swatted before he took his breakfast basket and vanished among the shrubbery. He called two minutes later from his own phone to ask if she was okay and did she miss him? Sarah said she was and did, and entertained herself with a few pleasant fantasies before she dropped off to sleep. This had not been exactly the best and worst of days, but it certainly had presented an interesting mixed bag.

CHAPTER 11

Sarah woke about half-past seven, phoned the carriage house to make sure Max hadn't overslept, was reassured by getting no answer, then set about preparing herself for the yachting party. There was a book of Alexander's she thought the Ganlors would like, to remember him by. It was time she began giving his things away. Bradley Rovedock ought to have a keepsake, too. She'd have to think of something appropriate.

But not today. The weather was going to be perfect, puffy clouds and just enough wind to make the cruise exciting without turning it into one of those all-hands-to-the-pumps affairs. Having sailed so seldom, and then only as a passenger, Sarah was not amused by watching the jib split or being told the rudder had carried away in a sudden squall.

She knew she wouldn't get seasick. At least she never had. Since she'd been lecturing Max on that very subject, though, she ate a sparing breakfast of tea and toast just in case. After that, she went down to make up Max's bed and found the empty thermos on his dresser with a few wild daisies stuck in it. They'd wilted because he'd forgotten to put any water in, but it was the sentiment that counted. She watered the poor things anyway, and took the thermos back to the big house with her.

Mr. Lomax and Pete weren't scheduled to come today, so she didn't have to worry about setting any tasks for them. She locked up carefully, got her sun hat, dark glasses, and windbreaker together, and was ready and waiting when Bradley arrived to pick her up.

Bradley drove the only Rolls Royce in Ireson Town. The Rolls was almost as much of a local landmark as the Kellings' 1920 Milbur used to be, except that it was much newer, infinitely more luxurious, and didn't need its batteries recharged every few miles. Alice B. had once tried to start a rumor that the car had been a gift from some Arabian potentate for whom Bradley had performed a great but secret service during his long wanderings. She hadn't got far, though. Nobody would credit the notion that Alice B. couldn't worm any secret from anybody given enough time and opportunity.

Bradley himself had laughed off her tale. He'd had a chance to pick up the car at roughly half price, he explained, and figured he'd be a fool to pass up the deal. Since a Rolls was built to last forever, more or less, he'd save in the long run by never having to buy another car. That made sense to the yacht club set, and everyone but Alice B. was satisfied.

Bradley was ahead of the game so far. After twelve years, the Rolls was still as good as new. One felt a sense of privilege to be riding in it. Bradley Rovedock did have that effect on people, Sarah thought as she settled herself on the sumptuous leather seat next to him. He could make one feel special without seeming to try. Certainly Bradley himself didn't make any attempt to be impressive, but he didn't have to. He simply was. Like Richard Corey, Sarah thought — then wondered why.

When they got to the yacht club, they found the Larringtons waiting on the dock. Lassie said, "Well, Sarah," and offered a limp handshake. Don said, "Well, Sarah," and got busy helping Bradley put the gear into *Perdita's* dinghy. Sarah began to wonder if she'd been wise to accept the invitation.

She wondered more when they'd rowed out to *Perdita* and found Fren Larrington already aboard. He gave her a helping hand out of the dinghy, though, and appeared ready to bury the hatchet. She wished that particular cliché hadn't come to mind, considering Alice B. and her lurid demise.

Anyway, he said, "Sorry we got our wires crossed last night," which was pretty magnanimous for Fren. Sarah replied that she hoped they'd had as good a time as possible under the circumstances. Then Bradley steered the conversation to marlin fishing, at which Don Larrington was the club's acknowledged expert, and the party began to liven up.

Lassie, showing them how at home she was aboard *Perdita*, went below to the galley and brewed a pot of coffee. Bradley turned over the helm to Fren and the sheets to Don, putting the twins in their glory, then brought up Peterson's guide and a pair of binoculars so that Sarah could study the sea birds. All Kellings were known to be avid bird watchers, though some of them had to pretend fairly hard in order to maintain the family reputation. Sarah happened to be among the genuinely interested. She welcomed both the diversion and the excuse not to make conversation with the Larringtons.

Bradley lounged beside her on the cockpit cushions, chatting about bananaquits and long-tailed tropic birds he'd seen during last winter's cruise. Once he snatched the binoculars from her thinking he'd spied a Franklin's gull which, according to Peterson, ought to be out somewhere around Minnesota. Then he realized it was only a laughing gull, as Sarah could have told him in the first place, and they both laughed with the gull.

They raised Little Nibble Cove about ten minutes ahead of what Bradley claimed had been his best running time to date. That set Fren and Don cock-a-hoop. Lassie demanded they celebrate by eating lunch before going ashore. Everybody was agreeable, knowing how transcendental the fare would be at the Ganlors'. Little Nibble, as Fren put it in a surprising burst of wit, was well-named. So they dropped anchor offshore and fetched up the picnic hamper.

Lunch was all Sarah had expected it

would be. She took her fair share, since the dry toast had worn off ages ago. Lassie did the serving.

"I'm so used to acting as hostess for Brad," she explained with a deprecating laugh. "You don't mind, Sarah?"

"Not in the least. Why should I? I love being waited on."

"Poor little Sarah." Bradley edged closer and topped up her glass of chablis. "They tell me you've been slaving for a houseful of — does one say paying guests?"

"One might, I suppose. We say boarders, ourselves. Actually I don't slave much any more. Cousin Brooks and his wife Theonia are taking over, and I have an incredible maid and butler who really run the show. In fact, right now I've let my own room and there's not even room for me in the house."

"What will you do next winter?"

Sarah felt a bit giggly. "Who knows? No thanks, Bradley, I've had far too much wine already. I might just trifle with one more of those heavenly almond cakes, though."

She might as well coddle herself while she had the chance. Sarah hadn't been used to luxuries. Her mother hadn't believed in coddling and her father had often appeared to forget she wasn't another grown-up with whom he was barely acquainted. He'd never sent his only child to school, but hired someone to come in and give her lessons. After his wife died, he'd taken it for granted that Sarah would handle the housekeeping. She'd been twelve then, with only a cook and a part-time maid to help her. Her father had died when she was eighteen and she'd married a fifth cousin some twenty years her senior, who was saddled with a blind mother and an old retainer who'd managed to dump most of her responsibilities on the young bride. Then her husband had been killed and she'd been left with a fresh set of burdens.

Now here she was, moderately solvent, relatively free, almost but not quite ready to marry a charming man with a lucrative though offbeat profession, eating French pastry on a millionaire's yacht. Despite the plague of relatives being visited upon her, despite the burned-out boathouse, despite a niggling suspicion that she was somehow mixed up in a particularly messy murder and robbery, Sarah had the distinct impression that she was happy.

She did wonder why Lassie Larrington kept eyeing her so oddly. No doubt Pussy

Beaxitt had already been on the phone giving Lassie an earful about last night. Maybe Lassie was surprised that Bradley'd still cared to have Sarah aboard *Perdita*. Or perhaps the crowd had got together and decided Walter's daughter was a brand to be snatched from the burning. It was an amusing concept. Sarah ate the last almond drop and announced that she for one was ready to go ashore.

"We can't go yet," Fren objected. "We haven't drunk all the wine."

"Want to heave anchor for me, Don?" was Bradley's only reply.

Don obviously did not want to do that or anything else except curl up on the cockpit cushions and sleep off his lunch, but he couldn't very well say so. He groped his way forward with his eyes half shut, managed the windlass deftly enough, and got the dripping flukes stowed in the bow. One thing about the yacht club crowd, Sarah thought, they did take their sailing seriously. She took pleasure in watching how deftly Bradley, taking the helm himself for this maneuver, set the big yacht right up to Little Nibble's long but somewhat tumbledown wharf.

He'd gone in under power, needless to

say. Docking under sail would have been more impressive but a lot riskier, and Bradley wasn't one to take chances. He looked dapper as a tern, Sarah thought, in a dark Greek fisherman's cap he'd picked up on his travels, a matching turtleneck jersey, and the white duck trousers that had been de rigeur for sailing when Bradley'd entered his first Beetle Cat in the children's races. Bradley had never since then worn anything but white ducks aboard and probably never would, even if he had to get them tailor-made at fabulous expense by now. One could not possibly imagine Bradley Rovedock in blue jeans.

Of all the Ireson crowd, he was the one who'd worn best. Sarah couldn't see that Bradley looked much different today than he had the first time she'd been aboard *Perdita*, back when her parents were both alive and Alexander, a young god in white ducks like Bradley's, had been kindly concerned to make sure little Sadiebelle got to hold the wheel for a few thrilling moments.

Granted she'd been more interested that day in the luncheon hamper than in the host who'd provided the goodies, but there'd been many more of these day cruises since then. Each year she'd seen

Alexander a shade older, a shade more care-worn while Bradley stayed about the same except for a few more sun wrinkles around the eyes and now, she noticed, brown blotches that were not freckles on the backs of his hands.

Sarah couldn't even notice any gray in Bradley's blondish hair when he took off the Greek cap to old Mrs. Ganlor. The doyenne of the island was sitting on the dock with her crabbing net and her falling-apart copy of Emerson's Essays, just as she'd been sitting every other time they'd come into Little Nibble Cove, wearing the same none-too-clean seersucker dress and the same droopy-brimmed, time-yellowed man's Panama hat she'd always worn. She rose to greet them with the same affable dignity Queen Elizabeth the First might have shown Sir Francis Drake when he returned from defeating the Spanish Armada.

"How kind of you to call, Bradley. Won't you come up to the mess hall? I think there's something left from lunch, though I can't recall what we had. If indeed I realized at the time."

"Thank you," he said, "but we lunched aboard *Perdita*. My cook, you know. She's sensitive about her prerogative as chief provider."

"Ah yes. She holds the power and bears the responsibility. Abraham Lincoln would have approved. But let me see whom you've brought with you. My other spectacles must be somewhere."

Mrs. Ganlor searched her pockets, then retrieved her glasses from the crabbing bucket, wiped off a few strands of seaweed, perched them on her nose, and peered at the little group behind Bradley.

"The Larrington boys, to be sure. How delightful to see you together. Now I shall have the visual stimulus of trying to tell you apart. No, you mustn't tell me. I'll have you sorted out in a moment."

Since Don was wearing his Porcellian tie over a paint-stained old sweatshirt, the sorting should not have been difficult; but Ganlors were not apt to be aware of sartorial details unless Thomas Carlyle had mentioned them first.

"And Lassie. I could never mistake you, my dear."

It was unthinkable that Mrs. Ganlor had ever watched an episode of that television program, but barely possible she might have dipped into Albert Payson Terhune during her frivolous infancy. Lassie did look much like her canine namesake with her long, pointed nose and mop of tawny hair. The hair was now streaked almost white around the face, either from exposure to sun and wind or because Lassie, like the rest of the crowd, wasn't getting any younger.

Alice B. had remarked only hours before her death that young pups tended to turn into old bitches and she'd been looking across the room at Lassie when she'd said it. They hadn't got around to discussing Alice B. yet, but they would, no doubt. Lassie hadn't talked much at all on the way over, but she'd chatter a blue streak all the way back. She always did. Even Alexander, who'd never been given to rude remarks, had observed the last time they'd been out in *Perdita* with Lassie and Don that he did wish Bradley had let sleeping dogs lie, Sarah remembered.

Mrs. Ganlor was remembering Alexander, too. She'd taken Sarah's hand in both of hers, a compassionate intimacy she'd never shown before. There might even have been a tear or two behind those kelp-clouded spectacles.

"Little Sarah. So young to have experienced such a loss. You will feel it less as you grow older, you know. One does.

'Time, like an everrolling stream, bears all its sons away.' Isaac Watts. Dear me, now where have I put down my reading glasses? There's a passage in Emerson — "

They knew better than to let Mrs. Ganlor get started on Emerson. Both Larrington brothers began talking at once. Lassie emitted a few preliminary yelps before Sarah, to her own surprise, captured the conversation. She began telling Mrs. Ganlor her adventures as a widow, eliminating the major troubles and making an amusing tale of her minor calamities; giving particular greetings from several aunts and imparting the interesting news that those two supposedly hopeless bachelors Dolph and Brooks were both happily married.

"Astonishing! 'The day shall not be up so soon as I, to try the fair adventure of tomorrow.' King John, Act Five, Scene One. One always does wonder whether it was really Shakespeare or Bartlett who wrote the plays, doesn't one? The best bits are all in the *Quotations*, and the rest is such a bore. But do come up and say hello to Josephus. He and I are the only ones around at the moment. Charlie and Willie have gone off to Lesser Nibble to look at a rock they're passionately excited about, though I'm afraid I can't remember why. It will come to me, sooner or later. Nobody else is on the island yet, though I expect the clan will start flocking any day now."

She was striding up the path as she talked, refusing to let anybody else carry her Emerson although she did entrust Don with the crabbing net and Fren with the bucket. Mrs. Ganlor must be eighty-five at least, Sarah thought, and her husband Josephus perhaps eight or nine years older. They found him mending a stone wall.

"Something there is that doesn't love a wall," was his predictable greeting. "In this case it was Grandfather Frost, I expect. Not related to Robert, so far as I know. In any event, one must get on with the job. 'For winter's rains and ruins are over.' "

"My dear, not Swinburne," his wife protested with a girlish laugh. "I'm sure you all remember that delicious passage in *Penrod* where the new minister is being entertained by the ladies of the neighborhood. 'A book of verse held lightly between the fingers.' Was that before or after Penrod poured glue into his hat? We thought we might use Tarkington for some of our reading aloud when the young people come out," she explained to her guests. "Sheer fluff, I know, but such fun. What do you think, Fren? You see I have you now."

The Fren she'd so confidently picked out happened to be Don, who couldn't recall any Tarkington except some chap who played football but wasn't about to confess that fact to Mrs. Ganlor. He said he thought Tarkington would be just the ticket.

Sarah, who knew her Tarkington back and forth from having spent so much time alone in her various relatives' libraries while her parents were visiting, put in a pitch for *Gentle Julia*.

"I adore that part where Julia lounges around eating candied violets and reading poetry about herself from a slim volume bound in limp purple suede," she sighed. "I always thought it would be lovely to have someone come courting me like that, but nobody ever did. I don't think I've even tasted a candied violet."

"I wouldn't know where to buy them now that the S.S. Pierce stores are out of business," mourned Lassie, pronouncing it "Purse" so that the Ganlors would know what firm she was talking about.

"Sage's Market in Harvard Square might have them," said Bradley. "I'll get my cook to call and find out. If they don't, I'll scour the seven seas to bring you some, Lady Sarah."

"And what about the book of poetry bound in limp purple suede?" Lassie inquired more cattily than doggily.

"As to that, she'll have to take the wish for the deed, I fear. What does rhyme with Sarah?"

Nobody could think of anything offhand, though Josephus gave it as his considered opinion that rhymes such as fairer and squarer might be allowable. "Especially since we in these parts do have that odd habit of omitting final 'r' except in words where it does not orthographically exist."

He hefted the large rock he'd been holding while they chatted and his wife took the hint.

"Come along, everyone. Let's go look for the goats and let this lazy man get back to his wall. Something there is that doesn't love a laggard and Josephus, poor dear, happens to be married to her. You must all be feeling cooped up after your sail. Nothing like a brisk canter over the moors to perk you up for the return voyage."

Fren and Don looked as if they could do without perking, but Lassie put her sharp nose to the trail and bounded off. Sarah was no less eager. She loved the moors and even liked the goats.

Years ago, the Ganlors had brought over a billy and a nanny with the idea of establishing thereby a ready source of milk and cheese. None of the family knew how to milk a goat, much less make cheese, but they'd had books along to teach them. The books, however, had not explained how one persuaded a goat to stand still long enough for one to practice on, and the animals themselves had not cooperated. They'd been too busy begetting more goats.

By now a sizable number of their descendants roamed Little Nibble. A walk on the moors was never less than a challenging experience. One might be tripped up by a group of frolicking kids, or knocked down by a charging billy goat. But, as Mrs. Ganlor always reminded their victims, they did keep down the poison ivy.

Sarah hoped they'd come upon one soon. She went hopping over the hummocks and boulders as though she'd been a kid again herself. Bradley Rovedock kept close to her the way Alexander used to do. She half expected to hear, "Watch out for a sudden charge, Sadiebelle," but Bradley wasn't saying anything. It occurred to her after a while that he might be having trouble catching his breath. She slowed her pace and Lassie forged ahead. A couple of minutes later, Lassie came running back.

"Mrs. Ganlor, I think one of your goats is in trouble. It's making an awful racket."

They all rushed after her as she led them to the source of the frenzied bleats. The goat was indeed in a bad way. A young male, it had somehow got its head and horns tangled in a roll of old barbed wire. In trying to pull free, it had gouged itself on the barbs. Blood was dripping down its front, staining the grass the goat must have been trying to reach when it was trapped.

Fren took one look, grunted, picked up one of the big lumps of granite that dotted the moor, and bashed the wretched beast's head in.

"Only thing to do," he told Mrs. Ganlor. "Might as well save the skin and meat. Tell Charlie and Willie to come out here and butcher it when they get back."

"Oh — yes, of course. One must be practical." Mrs. Ganlor was too much a philosopher to show how rattled she was, but Sarah felt sick to her stomach. Couldn't they at least have gone back for some wire cutters and freed the goat so they could make sure its wounds were really as bad as they looked? Did it have to be slaughtered so offhandedly as that?

Lassie didn't appear to mind, and Don was in full agreement with his brother, especially about leaving the corpse for the Ganlor sons to cope with. Bradley must have taken a good look at Sarah's face, though.

"Speaking of getting back," he said, "I've been wondering whether those clouds mightn't mean we're in for a tossing-around if we don't head for home port fairly soon. What do you think, everyone?"

"Tide and wind stay no man's pleasure," Mrs. Ganlor agreed. "Otherwise, we should be delighted to have you join us in partaking of the cup that cheers."

But does not inebriate. Even the Larringtons knew how that one came out. They agreed unanimously that it was surely coming on to blow and all hands ought to be on deck forthwith. The embarkation was speedy and efficient.

As soon as they'd worked *Perdita* clear of Little Nibble Cove, Fren remarked, "Phew! I could use a stiff one after that."

"I should think you might," Sarah answered none too amiably. "That poor goat!"

"What goat?" he grunted. "I meant the poetry."

"Lassie," said Bradley, "why don't you nip down to the galley, if you'll be so good, and bring up that smaller wicker hamper we left stowed in the starboard locker? There ought to be a thermos of hot rum toddy in it. One tends to feel a tad chilly after one's descent from the Elysian fields. At least I do. They are marvelous people though, aren't they?"

Everybody agreed the Ganlors were marvelous and the prospect of a hot rum toddy even more so. Lassie had an attentive audience as she unpacked the thermos jug along with a virgin tin of Bremner wafers, an assortment of cheeses ready sliced, a nest of plastic tumblers, and even a little pile of cocktail napkins with *Perdita's* quarterboard silk-screened on them, no doubt a gift from someone or other to the man who had everything.

Sarah took a rather skimpy tot of the rum. She'd have been content with the Ganlor's herb tea, but didn't say so because they must be thinking her pretty eccentric already. All except Bradley, bless him. He'd come over to sit with her again, now they were safely away from the island and Fren back at the helm with a drink in his spare hand.

"Happy, Sarah?"

"It's been a wonderful day."

"Then we must do it again soon. All but the goat, eh?"

Don reached across to see if there was anything left in the toddy jug. "Hell, is she being squeamish about that? What's another corpse or two in her young life?"

"You always were the soul of tact, Don," said his wife not very chidingly. "By the way, I wonder if they've come up with any word on Alice B. yet. You know, there was something awfully funny about that robbery."

"What's so funny about robbery, for God's sake? You want a little more of this before Fren swills it all?"

Lassie held out her glass. "I don't mean that kind of funny, idiot. I mean funny-peculiar. The sort of thing they took. I don't know if the rest of you happened to notice, but it was all paintings, that sort of thing. I mean, what thief would take a silly old etching and leave a diamond necklace?"

"What diamond necklace?"

"The one Miffy was wearing that afternoon, silly. That thing of her Great-aunt

169

Maud's. You know what I mean, she always puts it on when she has company. It's her notion of dressing up, like you and your stupid tie. She inherited the necklace, so she might as well get the good out of it, I suppose."

"So?"

"So Miffy told me yesterday she remembers taking the necklace off because it was pinching her neck or something, and putting it in that little crystal bowl on the table by the fireplace. She went to bed without remembering to take it out, for reasons I'm sure I don't have to explain, though of course she didn't go into that part. Anyway, when she started checking around after the robbery, there was the necklace right where she'd left it, but a watercolor that had been hanging over the table was gone."

"Who was the painter?" asked Sarah.

"Somebody named Millard Sheets, whoever he may be."

"An American painter of this century. Mrs. Jack Gardner collected some of his early work, as I recall."

"Worth stealing?" Don barked.

"Worth stealing, certainly. I can't imagine one watercolor would have anything approaching the resale value of Miffy's necklace, though."

Sarah knew what Lassie was talking about: a choker fully an inch wide, paved solid with diamonds, having a front clasp set with stones the size of peas and one rather staggering ruby in the middle. The thing was hideous to look at and must have been agony to wear, but she couldn't picture any thief passing up such a chance to get his hands on it.

"Unless they thought it was costume jewelry," she said. "Still — "

"What the hell, you'd stick it in your pocket just in case, wouldn't you?" said Don. "Lot easier than lifting a damn watercolor, I should think. What's the current market value of a what's-his-name?"

"I couldn't say offhand. Max will know."

"That's your boyfriend from the filling station?"

Even Lassie appeared to realize Don had gone too far this time. "At least he's heard of Millard Sheets," she snapped.

"Yeah, that's right." Fren took his eyes off the jib long enough to glance over at Sarah. "He's some kind of art dealer, isn't he? It is funny, now you mention it, that the pictures got pinched right after he'd been there to look 'em over."

"Fren," Bradley Rovedock was angry. "I'll take the helm now. How about getting the fenders overside?"

"Already? We're still quite a way from the mooring. Oh, I get it. You're being tactful. Sorry if I hurt your feelings, Sarah. But damn it, you hurt mine last night. I thought we were going to have a fun evening and you stood me up for a — okay, Brad, I'll get the fenders."

After that, the sail couldn't be over fast enough for Sarah. Bradley tried to keep the party alive and she did her best to respond out of politeness, but it had to be a brave effort. Fren wouldn't have thought of that business about Max himself. He must be repeating what others had been saying last night at the club.

And the more they said it, the more they'd believe it. Don's eyes were already narrowed, perhaps in speculation, perhaps in drowsiness. It didn't matter which. Don would side with his brother on general principles. Even Lassie, who'd been one of those clustered nearest to Max at Miffy's party, would be hissing like a teakettle about this latest tidbit when she got together with Pussy Beaxitt and the rest of the crowd tomorrow at the funeral.

Sarah told herself it didn't matter. She wasn't one of them any more. But as Max himself had said, she was. How could she give up the Ganlors, for instance? Insofar as tastes and manners went, they were as antithetic to the Larringtons as possible, but they were of the same breed. It was no use trying to pretend she could drop one without antagonizing the other. Anyway, there were kind people like Bradley Rovedock to bridge the gaps. When he asked if she'd like to take the helm for a minute, she smiled up at him.

"I'd love to. Remember how you always used to let me when I was a little girl?"

"Ouch! I remember all too well. I hoped you'd forgotten."

"How could I? That was always the most glorious part of going sailing with you. Oh dear, I'm getting a wrinkle in the jib."

"Ease her off a point. No, the other way or we'll jibe."

Sarah hastily corrected her error. "Dare I remind you about the time I did jibe and Mother spilled the tea basket right into Cousin Mabel's lap? How did you ever let Cousin Mabel aboard, anyway?"

Bradley was laughing now. "I believe she was visiting your people and I couldn't get out of it. You never did hit it off with that worthy lady, did you? I still have a hunch you dunked her on purpose.

"I'm sure I should have, if I'd been a good enough sailor."

"Now that you've got your hands on Walter's money, you ought to get yourself a nice little sixteen-foot sloop to learn on," said Fren, trying no doubt to make amends for his gaffe in the only way that came naturally to him.

Sarah wasn't buying either the apology or the sloop. "You're the one who was wailing to me about how much it costs to keep a boat."

"What doesn't cost these days?" growled Don. "Tell me that."

They finished the cruise convincing each other they'd all wind up in the poorhouse together and should they have dinner at the club or run up to Marblehead in Bradley's Rolls.

"I honestly can't," Sarah insisted. "After the flap I caused last night, I don't dare not go straight home. I've no idea whether Aunt Appie is still at Miffy's or waiting for me back at the house with a nice tuna fish casserole in the oven."

"But last night was different," Fren argued. "We expected you, damn it."

Bradley shook his head. "We'd better let Sarah decide what's best for her. Poor Appie does take her responsibilities seriously, doesn't she?"

"Hers and everybody else's," yipped Lassie.

"Whatever happened to Lionel and his four friends, Sarah?" asked Don, who must not have been asleep after all. "Understand you pitched them out bag and baggage after they burned down your boathouse."

"Wouldn't you? I wasn't about to have them roaming loose after that fiasco. Anyway, all their gear got wet from the fire hoses and they had nothing left to camp with. The last I saw of them, they were heading for the village laundromat to dry out."

"What's all this nonsense about Vare and Tigger?" Lassie wanted to know.

"You can probably answer that one better than I," Sarah replied, having little doubt that Lassie could. "All Lionel told me is that the two of them are living together and he's stuck with the boys. I don't know whether he and Vare are going to swap off from time to time, or what. The whole business is ridiculous in my opinion. I

175

daresay I did get rather savage about the fire, but I'm in such a ticklish position over that mortgage business that I felt I had to be."

"I can't picture you being savage about anything," Bradley murmured.

Lassie snickered. "Oh, Sarah's a changed woman these days."

"I keep telling everyone I'm not, but they won't believe me. Bradley, quick, there's the channel buoy. What shall I do now?"

"I'll take her."

He expertly twitched the wheel and steered *Perdita* into the safe channel without so much as causing the sails to flutter. All three Larringtons went into a flurry of crewmanship. Sarah, not knowing what else to do, repacked the cocktail hamper. By the time they'd picked up *Perdita's* mooring, everything was ship shape and they rowed back to the yacht club dock singing, "When you come to the end of a perfect day." Sarah sang along with the rest, but only because she knew Bradley would be hurt if she didn't.

CHAPTER 12

"Why don't we drop in at Miffy's for a quick one?" Fren suggested as they all got into Bradley's car. "Cheer her up."

"Are you crazy?" snorted his brother. "Alice B. isn't there any longer, in case you'd forgotten. Appie might have cooked something."

"Oh Christ, I never thought of that."

Fren wasn't thinking about that goat he'd killed, either. Sarah was glad when they dropped her off.

"Thanks so much, Bradley. I'm sorry I can't ask you all in for a drink, but there's hardly a drop in the house."

That was enough to get rid of them, as she'd known it would be. They waved and drove off. Sarah unlocked the side door and went in.

Appie was not in residence, she was infinitely relieved to find. She had the place to herself, and thank God for that. She felt totally done in. Too much sun and wind, too much to eat and drink, and decidedly too much of the Larringtons. Maybe a cup of tea would straighten her out. She'd put the kettle on in a minute. Right now, Sarah wanted most to lie down and see if she couldn't shake the feeling that the floor was rocking under her feet. She stretched out on the living room sofa. The next thing she knew, it was dark.

"I must have dropped off to sleep."

How odd. Sarah never took naps, as a rule. She was sorry she'd done so this time. Her head ached, she had a crick in her neck, a cramp in her leg, and a general feeling of loginess that didn't bode well for a peaceful night's sleep.

Maybe a walk would straighten her out. The breeze Bradley had predicted back on Little Nibble had come up. She could hear it panting down the chimney and rattling that loose board on the porch she'd been meaning to ask Mr. Lomax to do something about. Good, that meant there wouldn't be too many bugs around. She found an old poplin jacket her mother had left at Ireson's sometime or other and Sarah had adopted as her own years ago, pulled it on, and fastened the two remaining buttons.

As soon as she got outside, she put the hood up over her head, for the wind was even gustier than she'd anticipated. She'd better not risk the cliff path tonight. Alexander had preached at her often enough about playing safe. Sarah was small and lightly built. A strong blast might spin her off balance and send her staggering over the edge.

One might stroll past the carriage house, to see whether by chance Max had got back earlier than one expected he would. One did, but he hadn't, so Sarah kept going downhill through the pine grove. It was lovely here in the half-light that still lingered. Fragile white starflowers shone out bravely. Lady's slippers were harder to spot but welcome to see. They'd made a good recovery since that ghastly time some vandal had got in and picked most of them. Alexander would have been relieved. He'd worried terribly about the lady's slippers.

Now the ground was moister and she was getting into the hardwoods. Here ferns were more luxuriant, still not more than tallish green sticks, their tops curled like the violin section of an orchestra. Sarah could never see ferns in spring without thinking of Fridays at Symphony. She'd gone with her father all that first winter after her mother died because he'd paid for a pair of season's tickets and could hardly let them go to waste. The next year, however, he'd dropped his membership because he'd never cared much for music anyway. Since then, Sarah hadn't attended except when somebody had an extra ticket, which always seemed to be when they were playing Hindemith or Bartòk. Until lately.

Max adored classical music. He'd already taken her to several concerts. Maybe they'd have season's tickets again when they were married. It was when, not if. She was sure of that much by now, at least.

How utterly stinking of the Larringtons to be spreading that garbage about Max. They no doubt had their heads together now, deciding he must have gone off somewhere to dispose of his loot. They'd know he was out of town. Bradley Rovedock would have told them so, if Pussy Beaxitt hadn't beaten him to it. She'd have got that from Appie, and God alone knew what else since Appie had never once in her life managed to get her facts quite straight. Poor Aunt Appie must be having a dreadful time of it, not wanting to believe anything bad about Sarah's tenant and not willing to admit her friends could say he'd done something terrible if they didn't know it was true.

It was getting awfully dark here under the trees. Sarah had a flashlight with her, but it wouldn't do her much good if she got too far off the path and had to spend the night wandering among the poison ivy. The best thing to do would be to keep the wind on her right cheek and keep going downhill until she found the burned-out clearing where the boathouse used to be. Then she could follow the rutted track out to the drive.

She slogged on, picking blackberry vines away from her legs and wondering how she managed to keep getting herself into things. Gradually she became aware that she was hearing not only the soughing of the wind in the trees, but also human voices. Could Mr. Lomax and Pete have come back to finish taking down the boathouse? It wouldn't be the first time the caretaker had turned up at some unexpected time to complete a job, and this was a busy time of year for him.

But why were there so many different

voices, and why did they sound so young? Had Pete brought his kids with him? Or was it — she froze in horror, then went grimly forward. One might as well face the worst. Cousin Lionel was back.

"Oh there you are, Sarah," was her cousin's joyful greeting. "Where were you earlier? I wanted Alex's hatchet and that man of yours wasn't around to get it for me. Why didn't you leave the tool shed unlocked?"

"Because I didn't want people like you wandering in and swiping the tools," she responded with equal cordiality. "Whatever are you up to?"

"Building a lean-to, as I should have thought you could observe for yourself. That's right, Woody. Shove the pointed end of the upright well into the ground before you lash it to the crosspole."

"The end isn't pointed, dummy."

"Then we'll point it, shall we?"

Lionel had managed to get a hatchet from somewhere. Deftly as though he were sharpening a pencil with a jackknife, he struck neat scallops from the end of the two-inch sapling his son was holding, whittling it into a perfect point. "There you go, Woody."

"Hey, not bad."

For once, Lionel appeared to be commanding some respect from his band of ruffians. He'd got them to dig a businesslike firepit, well-ringed with stones to keep their campfire from getting out of control in this wind. The lean-to they were building was a professional-looking affair with a framework of lashed-together poles against which they were erecting a latticework of unpeeled saplings.

"Tomorrow we're going to thatch the poles with overlapping branches of evergreen," Lionel explained. "For tonight we'll simply stretch a segment of our tent across the framework. The part that didn't get burned," he added accusingly.

"Don't snarl at me," Sarah told him. "I didn't set that fire. Where do you think you're going to get water?"

"From the well, of course. We've uncovered it and constructed a well-sweep with a rope and bucket to draw up the water. Show her, Jesse."

"It's my turn," yelled little Frank.

"Aw, you couldn't even lift the bucket," said his loving brother. "You can show her the latrine."

For a child of his years, Frank had a remarkable vocabulary. He spent some time explaining in detail to Jesse precisely what he could do with the latrine before he did in fact take Sarah to view their new sanitary facility. Situated well away from the camp and, she was glad to see, downhill from the water supply, it was a sort of tepee made from more saplings, another fragment of tent, and a sawhorselike seat straddling a deep trench. There was even a can of chloride of lime.

"That's to keep down the stink," James told her.

"How nice," said Sarah. "Let's go over to the well."

She was dreadfully concerned about that, but she needn't have been. Lionel hadn't merely taken off the cover and left a gaping hole for some playful son to shove a sibling into. He'd erected a fence of stout poles deeply planted, reinforced with piles of rock, and laced together with willow withes. The fence was too high for the boys to climb over without stupendous effort, and the poles were sharpened at the tops to discourage temptation.

The well-sweep was so ingeniously contrived that Sarah had a hard time believing Lionel had thought of it. Moreover, it worked. Jesse proved that by drawing a pailful of water and dumping it over Frank's head. Frank lisped out several more words Sarah had never heard before.

"That will do, lads," said their father genially. "Frank, why don't you skin out of those wet clothes and caper around the campfire Indian-style until you're warmed up? Then on with the pajamas and into the old sleeping bag, eh?"

Frank made a suggestion about the old sleeping bag but, oddly enough, did as he was bidden.

"You're not going to let that fire burn all night, I trust?" Sarah said to her cousin.

"I see no need. The lean-to will be quite snug and I have succeeded in getting our sleeping bags completely dry. It cost me two dollars and seventy-five cents in quarters," Lionel added in an aggrieved tone.

"Hard cheese. Heaven only knows what this boathouse fire is going to cost me when the bank gets wind of it."

"Sarah, I am in no mood to concern myself with other people's money problems."

By now all four of his sons were capering around the campfire Indian-style, getting covered with soot from the fire-blackened grass, making the night hideous with their yells, and having a thoroughly educational time. Lionel hunkered down on a log, picked up a stick of pine about a foot long, swiped the bark from it with four neat sweeps of his hatchet, and began turing it into a fuzz stick, cutting thin shavings perhaps an inch deep diagonally into the wood and leaving their ends attached so that they curled back and gradually gave the stick the look of a toy Christmas tree.

"Do you know what this latest insanity of Vare's is costing me?" he demanded. "I've had to hire a full-time housekeeper, for one thing. You wouldn't believe what those people have the audacity to charge."

Considering what this one would have to put up with, Sarah thought, no salary whatever could possibly be large enough. She didn't say so, though. She was rather horribly fascinated by the way that heavy hatchet was peeling back those delicate shavings with never a slip.

"And Vare's making ridiculous claims about her allowance. That ghastly Tigger's fastened on to her like a leech. I'm supporting the pair of them in luxury while they sit around drinking gin fizzes and laughing about what a fool they've made of me. But that's going to be all over at the end of this week. I told Vare last night I was through shelling out for her and that anthropoid she's taken up with."

He threw down the fuzz stick and slammed the hatchet into the log so violently that Sarah jumped up in alarm. Lionel, always so controlled, was in a boiling rage. She hadn't thought it could happen but there was the hatchet, its blade half buried in the log altogether too close to where she'd been sitting.

"And there'll be all the school fees coming up in a couple of months." His sons, even little Frank, went to highly progressive and correspondingly expensive private schools, of course. "Tuition will be raised again, no doubt, like everything else. And God knows what the taxes will be on Father's estate if it ever gets settled. I'll be lucky if I don't wind up having to support Mother on top of everything else. And you know what shape the stock market's in these days."

Sarah didn't know, but she judged the shape couldn't be good. So Lionel was feeling the pinch, too, and apparently with reason. It occurred to her all of a sudden why Lionel was so unexpectedly handy with the hatchet. He and Vare had spent their honeymoon doing one of those survival programs where each got dropped into a separate patch of trackless wilderness equipped only with two matches, a compass, and an axe. Some of the family, notably Uncle Jem, had expressed regret when they'd both come out more or less unscathed.

Both Lionel and Vare had gone in heavily for self improvement, even after they'd discovered procreation. Sarah recalled having bumped into Vare one day over at the Busch Reisinger Museum in Cambridge, while Jesse was a drooling lump in a canvas sack on his mother's back and Woody still only a lump under her poncho.

"I'm exposing them to the aesthetic experience," Vare had explained.

Nor was she tryng to be funny. Vare wouldn't know a joke if it walked up and bit her on the ankle.

"But the one in the bag is asleep and the other hasn't even been born yet," Sarah had protested.

"I did not say I was teaching them," Vare had corrected. "I said I was exposing them. Subliminally, you know. When the time comes to begin conscious enrichment of their understanding, Lionel and I will introduce them to a variety of artistic stimuli by means of slides, books, lectures, and direct encounter. We are already taking refresher courses in art history on the nights when we don't do yoga or canoe building."

So Lionel ought to know a Fantin-Latour when he saw one, not to mention a Millard Sheets. Would it be so very unlike Lionel to commit an art robbery with the object of repairing his fractured finances, and ignore a diamond necklace because it didn't happen to be on his list of things to steal?

It would be much more like Vare. Maybe she and Tigger had decided to acquire a richer experience of grand larceny.

That wasn't funny, either. Sarah found she could easily believe something like that of Vare. Everything her cousin and his wife had ever done, from the survival-camp honeymoon to the rapidfire production of Jesse, Woodson, James, and Frank, had been far more Vare's doing than Lionel's. She'd bet anything it had been Vare's idea to park her husband and sons on Sarah for the summer. Vare would assume they'd have no trouble taking over and running things to suit themselves now that Alexander wasn't around to put the brakes on.

Vare hadn't been so far wrong, either. Sarah'd thought she was rid of them and here they were, settled in as if nothing had happened. The worst of it was, now they'd put in all this work making the supposedly ruined campsite not only livable but down-right homey, Sarah knew she wouldn't have the heart to turn them out again. Not until catastrophe struck again, anyway, as it doubtless would. She went around to the end where the hatchet wasn't and sat down again beside Lionel.

"Where are Vare and Tigger living now?"

"They've taken a place on Chauncy Street in Cambridge."

"So close to you and the boys?"

"Where else would they go? Vare's still taking courses at Harvard, you know."

Sarah hadn't known, but she might have guessed.

"She had her summer schedule all mapped out before she decided to do this absurd thing with Tigger. She could hardly change that."

"I don't see why not, when she was chang-ing everything else. Whatever prompted her to — " Sarah faltered. This was too much like the sort of question Alice B. would have asked. "I'd had the impression you and Vare had worked out a thoroughly via-ble lifestyle," she substituted, choosing the sort of phraseology Lionel would be most apt to understand.

"So had I," he responded gloomily. "Dash it, Sarah, I cannot for the life of me understand why she's treating me this way. I've always done everything she — that is to say, Vare and I had always explored the ramifications and arrived at a joint resolution on any course of action. But when this Tigger lunacy came up, she absolutely refused to enter into any sort of rational discussion. She wouldn't even listen to me. I — "

He glanced over to make sure his sons were too engrossed in their own caterwauling to overhear. "I raised my voice. Sarah, I haven't told this to anybody else, not even Mother, but I lost my temper. I honestly believe if I'd had this hatchet in my hand at that moment — but this is idle conjecture."

Lionel took a few deep breaths, then managed to speak more calmly. "Sarah, what would be your thoughts with regard to the boys' attending Alice B.'s funeral tomorrow?"

"Tomorrow? Oh dear, it is, isn't it? I suppose I'll have to show up, or your mother will have kittens again. But I don't think you should take the boys, Lionel."

She could think of nothing more dire than sitting through a service with Jesse, Woody, James, and Frank erupting all around her. Lionel, naturally, was thinking along different lines.

"Modern psychiatric emphasis is strongly on the necessity for learning to cope with the death experience. This would give them an opportunity to get in some practice."

"At the funeral of a murder victim? Lionel, I do think that's a bit much. Besides, they've already coped when your father died."

After the obsequies, it had been the consensus that the prospect of never having to put up with his grandsons again must have made death a welcome release for Uncle Samuel. Sarah could picture Miffy going into raging hysterics all over the church if they got a chance to try on their antics at Alice B.'s funeral.

"But Vare said — "

"When did Vare say? Alice B. only got killed night before last."

"I spoke with her last night. The boys and I had to go back to Cambridge, as you should have realized, since other hospitality was not forthcoming."

"You could have gone to a public campground."

"And fork out some outrageous fee to be crowded in with a pack of God-knows-whats? I'd already had to spend all that money at the laundromat. Anyway, I knew Vare would be planning to attend the funeral, so I decided I might as well call her up and discuss the matter with her."

"Why should Vare come to the funeral?"

"Because Alice B. was her aunt, of course."

Sarah gasped. "Lionel, I'd completely forgotten. Vare was a Beaxitt, wasn't she?"

"She still is. Rather, she has resumed her maiden name, if the term is still in use."

"Then she's also related to Biff and Pussy."

"To Biff, certainly. They are first cousins once removed. It was Biff's wife Pussy, in fact, who may be said to have brought Vare and me together."

"Then if Pussy gets axed to death next, we'll know whom to blame."

"I trust, Sarah, you meant that as a witticism."

However, Lionel looked thoughtful as he pulled the hatchet out of the log and added a last row of curls to his fuzz stick.

CHAPTER 13

Sarah left her cousin sitting on the log and walked back out to the drive, wishing she could meet Max coming back and hear him tell her not to be silly. Why did Lionel have to be so handy with a hatchet? Why did he have to choose tonight to engage for the first time in his life in cousinly confidences about his marital problems, his financial woes, and his slipping self-control? Why had he reminded her Vare was a niece of Alice B., and why did he have to be so damned psychologically oriented? If Lionel was able to admit he'd come that close to killing Vare, Sarah wouldn't put it past him to decide he should displace his hostilities in a sane and healthy manner by butchering Vare's aunt instead.

And what about Alice B.'s money? If there was no will, then Vare ought to come into something, along with Biff Beaxitt. If there was, Vare was more likely than Biff to be mentioned because of Alice B.'s feud with Pussy over the garnet jewelry.

Lionel himself didn't stand much chance of getting anything, but he'd benefit indirectly if Vare were to inherit. Then he'd have a legitimate excuse not to pay her any more allowance. Sarah put little stock in his assertion that he'd put a stop to that. She knew Vare too well, and so did he.

As to having known what to steal, both Vare and Lionel ought to qualify, and not just because of their art courses. They'd been in and out of Miffy's house often enough to know every stick in it, not because Miffy wanted them there but because Appie's son and Alice's niece had to be tolerated regardless. They'd have felt duty-bound to pay attention to the works of art it contained. With Lionel, appreciation and appraisal would go hand in hand as a matter of course.

Vare was no slouch when it came to current market values, either. She read the consumer reports. She did her grocery shopping with a miniature calculator in her hand, and woe to the supermarket cashier who came up with a different total than Vare's.

Lionel was, after all, Sarah's own cousin and Aunt Appie's only son. Sarah couldn't help not wanting him to have got himself involved with something he'd surely get caught for. Lionel was a great planner, but his logic always had a flaw in it somewhere. Anyway, of the two, Vare did seem the likelier suspect.

In the first place, she'd stuck Lionel with their sons. If he'd tried to sneak out on them the night of the murder, one or the other of the boys would surely have found out and ratted on him, they being the little dears they were. Besides, Vare had Tigger to help her. That would go along with Sarah's theory about two people being involved. If Tigger's looks and manner were any clue to her proclivities, a spot of bloody mayhem ought to be right up Tigger's alley.

To be sure, there was always the possibility Lionel and Vare had done it together. They might have gone through this splitting-up act for the express purpose of putting the police off their scent. That did seem pretty farfetched. Lionel had sounded awfully sincere in his lamentations just now.

But why pick on Lionel just because he was good at making fuzz sticks with a hatchet? What about Fren Larrington, who had a rotten temper and didn't mind bashing hurt animals over their heads with rocks? Fren was no doubt in the same boat as Lionel, with a divorced wife demanding alimony. Who wouldn't expect to be lavishly compensated for having put up with Fren all those years?

How could Fren pull off such a selective robbery, though? He didn't know thing one about art. And what if he didn't? His sister-in-law was Pussy Beaxitt's tennis partner and willing ear. It was a safe bet Lassie knew to the penny how much every last thing in Miffy's house was worth. Pussy would have made it her business to find out, and pass the word along. Lassie would have told Don, who loved hearing about large sums of money in any context, and Don would have told Fren because Fren was his twin.

The corollary to that was, if Fren had been the robber, then Don had been his helper. He'd have been the one who stood outside, taking the loot and coaching Fren about what to steal next. Sarah could see Fren moving handily around Miffy's cluttered house as he'd done today on *Perdita's* deck. As he'd done in Sarah's own kitchen yesterday morning, come to think of it, helping himself to what he wanted without so much as a by-your-leave, and chiding her for not keeping a more shipshape galley.

Not stealing Miffy's diamond necklace would be characteristic of Fren, too. He was a good crewman, used to taking orders. If Don had told him to take the painting by the fireplace, he wouldn't even have bothered to glance at what might be on the table below, but simply gone and got the painting.

Fren would have killed Alice B., too, if Don handed him the axe and told him to do it. Once she'd spotted the Larrington brothers committing a robbery, there could have been no question of leaving Alice alive to tell.

That alleged invitation to the yacht club could have been Don's idea, also. The way Fren had delivered it smacked more of an errand boy doing a job than of a single man yearning for feminine companionship. No doubt he had been annoyed when Sarah didn't show up after he'd gone to the bother of asking her, but that could be because she'd been supposed to be part of some elaborate alibi they were concocting.

Maybe Don and not Fren had instigated the robbery on his own behalf. Don was an investment counselor, and Lionel said the market was doing strange things. He might have some customers wanting to put their money into tangible assets, and what could be better than works of art? Better still, why not steal the Paintings himself, sell them to his clients, take a hundred per cent profit on the sales, and not pay a cent of income tax? Don could even have convinced himself it wasn't such a terrible thing to do, because he knew Miffy had everything insured right up to the hilt. She'd be reimbursed, and never have to pay any more premiums. That Miffy might like the things for their own sake would never occur to him.

Could one get away with a scheme like that? Max would know. She did wish he'd come home. Sarah walked back to the carriage house, but there was still no sign of him. The sensible thing would be to go back and climb into bed, but she still wasn't sleepy after her nap, and she did have qualms about being alone in the main house when Max wasn't within calling distance. That little business of the lights still bothered her. Why hadn't she done the sensible thing today and got the electrician, instead of letting herself in for a day with the Larringtons?

But it hadn't been just the Larringtons. There'd been Bradley, and the Ganlors, and the joy of being on the sea. Maybe she could get down to the water's edge now. The wind didn't seem to be gusting so hard. She picked her way to the long wooden staircase and used her flashlight to guide her down to the beach.

The tide was dead low, the sky was clear. This would have been a perfect night for stargazing, but she'd better concentrate on where she was walking. It wouldn't do to turn an ankle on the slippery rocks. Alexander'd have had seven fits in a row if he'd known she was down here by herself at night.

Under the cliff, there was more shelter from the wind. Sarah could feel her mind flattening out, her whole self becoming attuned to the soothing lap of the water against the gravel. This was the first time she'd been here since Alexander was killed. She was coming to what they'd used to call her wishing rock, where the two of them had sat squeezed together in loving embrace that last morning, making plans for a future that hadn't come. She'd thought she could never bear to go near the rock again. Tonight, it didn't hurt at all.

Sarah climbed up to the scooped-out seat where she'd spent so much time when she was a little girl making believe she could see mermaids riding white sea horses. There weren't any mermaids. That was gone, the pretending, the longing, the planning. Alexander was gone, too. The love was still with her, but the man was somewhere else, set free of this life forever and ever.

Now Sarah was free, too, and there was no sense in shillyshallying any longer. She walked back to the steps and hauled herself up by the handrail, bending double as the wind hit her. She took out her house keys, went to Max's apartment, and unlocked the door. She took off her clothes and lay down in his bed.

If Max had been here, she might not have acted so boldly. Then again, she might have. Sarah wasn't thinking at all now, just doing what felt right. The bed seemed warmer than her own. Being around Max always gave her that sense of warmth. Nice to know it worked even when he wasn't with her. She was smiling into the dark when she fell asleep.

Something woke her, she didn't know what. Maybe that was Max now, just coming into the carriage house. But why was he puttering around down there so quietly? Max could move silently when he wanted to, but he was more apt to come leaping up the stairs two at a time. Had he dropped his keys?

What if he had? There was no need to grope around in the dark. He knew there was a light switch just inside the door, and another by the staircase. Sarah hadn't bothered to turn them on herself because she'd had her flashlight, but why didn't he? She knew he hadn't because no gleam was showing through the crack under the door.

Perhaps a fuse had blown. What if it had? Max always carried a small pocket flash and had a powerful battery lantern in his car. Furthermore, if he'd run into any such minor inconvenience it wasn't like him to suffer in silence. Was he drunk? Maybe she'd better —

Maybe she'd better not. That wasn't Max downstairs. It might be an animal that had wandered in if she'd forgotten to shut the outside door, though she was pretty sure she'd remembered. It might be the trickster who'd planted that Bilbao looking glass in her front entry, or the fiend who'd hacked Alice B. to death, or both in one person. Most likely it was one of Lionel's brats

being cute. Sarah could imagine the reper-
cussions if he were to catch her here in
Max's bed with no clothes on. She only
hoped he wasn't setting fire to the place,
but she couldn't take the chance of getting
up to find out.

She didn't smell smoke, anyway. Sarah
lay there in the bed that didn't feel cozy
any more, not daring to move until she
heard the stealthy closing of a door and a
tiny rattle of gravel on the drive outside.
She waited perhaps ten minutes longer just
in case the intruder took a notion to come
back, but heard nothing. At last she eased
herself out of bed, retrieved enough of her
scattered clothes to be decent, put them on
any way she could, and opened the upstairs
door inch by inch.

Nobody was down there now. The place
felt empty, and was. Sarah switched on
every light she could find and started
checking around, particularly for any sign
of attempted arson. She'd got her head into
one of the old mangers when the door
opened again.

"What the hell's going on?"

That was Max, thank God. She rushed
out of the stall.

"It's me, darling. I was just making sure

nothing's on fire."

"Why should it be?"

"I heard somebody, or something. You didn't meet anyone on the drive?"

"To tell you the truth, I was too beat to notice. What a day! I ran my legs off from one end of New York to the other. Coming back we had to circle the airport for half an hour, don't ask me why. To put the frosting on the cake, a car broke down in the Sumner Tunnel just ahead of me and blocked both lanes, don't ask me how. There I was halfway under Boston Harbor breathing pure carbon monoxide and wondering when the roof was going to cave in on me. Then coming up the road here, some clown cut in front of me and damn near sliced my headlights off."

"Are you sure he didn't come out of our drive?"

"How can I be sure of anything? All I can tell you is, he was going like hell. What is this, anyway? How come you're down here at this hour?"

Sarah flushed. "I was up in the apartment, if you want to know."

"Doing what?"

"Waiting for you. Just — resting. I heard something moving around down here, and it scared me for a while, that's all. I was afraid it might be one of Lionel's boys setting another fire."

"I thought you'd got rid of them."

"So did I, but they're back. They've built a lean-to, a latrine, and a well-sweep."

"My God."

He shifted his briefcase to the other hand and put his arm around her. "So you were waiting for me. Come back upstairs and tell me about it."

It was a tight squeeze getting up that fretwork staircase with their arms around each other, but they managed. Max switched on the light and noticed the crumpled bed.

"Just resting, eh?"

He bent to pick up the brassiere she hadn't been able to find during her scramble to get dressed in the dark. "Feel like resting some more?"

"It's time, Max."

CHAPTER 14

She would have to pick the night he'd got stuck in the tunnel, Sarah moaned to herself half an hour later, while her allegedly importunate swain slumbered peacefully at her side. Well, you won some and you lost some. It was lovely just to be lying here snuggled against his body. She might as well shut her eyes and enjoy it.

Then the birds were chirping and the sun was shining in because neither of them had thought to draw the blinds. The watch that was the only thing Max had forgotten to take off said half past seven. Mr. Lomax would be coming at eight, and Sarah hated to think what might already be going on down at the campground.

So much for la dolce vita. She slid out of bed without disturbing Max, put her clothes on once more, and sneaked back through the bushes to the big house. She made it in time to be showered and changed by the time the Lomaxes arrived, but it was a near squeak.

"Where's my old buddy?" was Pete's cheerful greeting. "I thought we might talk baseball a while."

"I thought you might mend the drive while your uncle weeds the garden."

Sarah didn't at all care for the way Pete was smirking at her. What if it had been he prowling inside the carriage house last night? She wouldn't put it past him. And what if he hadn't gone away afterward, but hidden outside long enough to observe what went on before Max remembered to turn out the light?

She turned away so he wouldn't see her blushing. "Be sure you fill that big pothole by the boathouse path. The pumper almost got stuck in it yesterday. Don't just dump in some dirt, either. Use good, heavy rocks so they won't get washed away."

"Yeah, sure. Say, did you know them kids was back?"

"Certainly I knew. Mr. Lomax, would you unlock the tool shed and let Pete get out a wheelbarrow and shovel? I want that hole fixed right away."

The old man touched the peak of his cap and glared his nephew into submission. Sarah put on the coffeepot and was getting out spoons and forks when her demon lover blew in.

"Ran out on me, eh?" He rubbed his freshly shaven cheek against hers. "Couldn't you have stuck around till I'd got some rest?"

She shook her head. "Mr. Lomax was coming. Max dear, I really don't think I'm cut out for success as a femme fatale. There's always too darn much else going on. Would you mind terribly if we slipped off quietly and got married instead?"

"Not at all. When did you have in mind?"

"I thought we might pick up the license tomorrow, if you're free."

"What's wrong with today?"

"I have to go to Alice B.'s funeral."

"That's a hell of a reason. I suppose you want me to take you."

"If you can spare the time. Otherwise, I'm sure I could get a lift with Bradley Rovedock."

"The hell you will. You're mine. Mine, do you hear me? Mine!"

"Then quit trying to crack my ribs and

tell me what you want for breakfast. Oh, wouldn't you know. I'll get it. That must be Aunt Appie."

Sarah went to answer the phone. It was Appie in a dither, as she'd expected.

"Sarah dear, I wanted to remind you about the funeral. It's at ten o'clock, you know."

"Ten? Lassie told me eleven."

Was that an honest mistake, or did Lassie mean for her to miss the service and lose a few brownie points with Bradley? Could she actually have minded that much about Sarah's being included in the yachting party? She'd be further disappointed today, then. Sarah wasn't about to upset Aunt Appie for the sake of appeasing Lassie Larrington.

"It's all right, I'll be there. Do you need anything from your luggage?"

"Thank you dear, but I'm already togged out in my brown crepe. Alice B. used to tell me how much she liked it."

Alice B. had never failed to comment on that weary old dress. What she'd meant was, "For heaven's sake, aren't you ever going to buy a new one?" but Appie was too sweetly dense to realize she'd been insulted.

"Now Sarah, don't you worry about a thing. It's all arranged. Just get ready and Fren Larrington will be along to pick you up."

"Aunt Appie, I don't want Fren to pick me up. I'm going with Max."

"Max? You mean that young man from the — but Sarah, we have it all arranged."

"Forget it, Aunt Appie. Max and I have our own arrangement."

She raised her eyebrows at him. He nodded and she took the plunge. "It's going to be a permanent one."

"What, dear? I'm afraid I don't quite — "

"I mean Max and I are going to get married. This week, if we can manage it."

"Sarah! We all thought it would be so much nicer if you and Fren — "

"Max and I will see you at the church."

Sarah hung up the receiver. "Poor Aunt Appie. Maybe that will cure her of making nice little arrangements. How about toast and scrambled eggs? We haven't time for much else. I've got to change into something respectable, and I suppose you should put on a jacket and tie. Half of them will show up in jogging suits or tennis shorts, but we may as well set an example. We needn't stay on after the service."

That was more easily said than done. By the time Alice B. had been preached over in the little fieldstone church that served the summer colony and interred in the cemetery nearby, Aunt Appie was in an advanced state of the weeps. Sarah hadn't the heart to desert her, especially since Lionel had stayed back at the camp with the boys and Vare, though present, was making no effort to be civil. Max, with his well-developed sense of family solidarity, was quite willing to go along back to Miffy's if Sarah thought they should.

Miffy herself was bearing up surprisingly well. She'd even had sense enough to get in a local catering outfit to handle the drinks and the food, which turned out to be mostly things like chocolate chip cookies and dull chicken salad sandwiches with the crusts imperfectly trimmed. The cuisine was going to be far less interesting around here now that Alice B. was gone. Also the conversation, no doubt.

At least Sarah and Max were giving them something to talk about today. Startled glances were being directed their way. Max must be realizing what people would be saying, and either not giving a hoot or managing to look as if he didn't. Why should he?

Sarah certainly didn't.

It was Vare and Tigger who stole the show, however. This was not a dressy gathering, by and large — Aunt Appie's brown crepe was by no means the tackiest outfit present — but Tigger's cumbersome hiking boots, dirty corduroys, and hairy poncho did seem a bit much. As always, Tigger wasn't saying a word, just lurking in a corner and glaring at anybody who tried to approach her.

"You know," Sarah murmured to Max, "I wouldn't put anything past that woman. If that's what she is."

"Looks like a psycho to me," he agreed. "I hope your cousin's wife realized what she was getting herself into."

"I doubt it."

Vare had shown up in a man's dark gray pinstriped three-piece suit with a black four-in-hand tie and a starched white shirt. Her notion of what the well-dressed lesbian should wear to a favorite aunt's funeral, no doubt. The suit did not fit. It must be one of Lionel's. Suspecting that a real lesbian would be more inclined to wear whatever was becoming and appropriate, Sarah decided Vare was merely exploring another experience. She'd be back with Lionel and the boys, most likely, as soon as she'd had enough of Tigger.

Assuming Tigger would let her go. Watching that sullen face under the tangle of unwashed black hair, Sarah wasn't at all sure Vare was going to get away without a struggle. According to Lionel, Tigger was doing nicely out of the present arrangement, playing Vare for all her husband was worth. Would she be amenable to letting the gravy train roll off without her?

Miffy was not making the pair welcome. She ignored Tigger, walked up to Vare, took a long look at the three-piece suit and the black necktie, then snorted.

"Well, well. What have we here? I thought I'd seen the last of you, Vare, now that Alice isn't around to revel in your devotion."

"My interest in Aunt Alice was wholly sincere," Vare replied without a flicker of emotion.

"I don't doubt that for a moment. Interest and dividends both, not to mention the principal. Now that you're here, you might as well have a drink. I'm going to."

Miffy turned and strode over to the bar the caterers had set up. Vare, still poker-faced, followed her and took a glass of tomato juice. That must have been Aunt Appie's contribution. Miffy would never think to provide anything nonalcoholic.

Lassie was standing nearby. Sarah went up to her.

"I hadn't realized Vare was in the habit of visiting Alice B."

"That's because you're never around. Vare's been haunting the place for quite a while now, though she did have sense enough not to bring that creature with her until today, of all times to pick. Never brought her own whelps either. I expect she realized she herself was about as much as Alice B. could take. Vare's no fool, you know, even if she does act like a jackass more often than not."

Vare was, after all, Sarah's cousin-in-law. She wasn't about to start bending Lassie Larrington's ear about Lionel's wife's shortcomings.

"I know," she said. "Vare's terribly bright, actually. I've never met anyone keener on self-improvement."

"You can say that again. Especially when it comes to improving her financial position. She did everything but write Alice B.'s will for her."

Then there was a will. This was interesting, though Sarah tried to pretend it wasn't.

"But why should she bother? Not that it's any business of mine, but I always thought of Alice B. as — well, not exactly an employee but a sort of companion-help to Miffy. I assumed her cooking and what-not was a way of earning her keep."

Lassie took a swig from her glass. "Alice B. earned her keep all right, but not because she had to. Her own little nest was pretty well feathered. In my opinion, a few people are going to get quite a surprise when the will's probated."

"Really?" said Sarah. "Then I hope from a purely selfish family point of view that Vare does come in for something. You can imagine the sort of financial burden Lionel's carrying now with four boys to educate and all this hoo-ha going on."

She could see no sense in pretending it wasn't, when Vare and Tigger were taking such pains to let everybody know it was. "And you know what Don was telling us yesterday about the stock market," she threw in for good measure.

"Don't remind me," Lassie yipped. "I get the stock market every day of my life for breakfast and dinner, not to mention cocktail time. God, these Bloody Marys are flat. Appie must have made them."

"I expect you've got hold of a glass of plain tomato juice," Sarah told her. "That's what I'm having."

The look of horror on Lassie's face was almost worth having come to see. She slammed down the glass on one of Miffy's pearwood tables and hared off to the bar, leaving Sarah to remove the glass before it left a white ring, and to wonder about Vare.

She wished Max had been beside her to hear what Lassie'd said, but he was trapped by Pussy Beaxitt, who was doubtless trying to pry out of him the lurid details of his and Sarah's courtship. Sarah's lips twitched. There weren't all that many, even counting last night. Pussy wouldn't have got much out of Max in any case.

Aunt Appie was still red around the eyelids but nobody else appeared to be mourning Alice B. By now, the rest of them had evidently forgotten what they were supposed to be here for and turned the gathering into just another of Miffy's parties.

Miffy herself was going right along with the crowd. She was standing beside Pussy, grilling Max with the zest of a prosecuting attorney facing a hostile witness. Lassie, having equipped herself with two martinis, one in each hand, drifted over to the group. Almost everybody else, not excepting Vare and, for a wonder, Tigger, was doing the same. Even Bradley Rovedock was among them, though his motive must have been to urge a decent restraint because Sarah heard Miffy yap at him, "Shut up, Brad. Don't be such a damned old maid."

The crowd shifted. Sarah caught a glimpse of Miffy reaching down to tug at the stockings she'd put on for the occasion. This was the first time in her life Sarah'd ever seen those hairy, knotted old legs so demurely covered. When it was paralyzingly cold, Miffy wore woolen pants and rubber boots with heavy socks inside them. Most of the time, she slopped around in nothing more than a battered pair of rawhide sandals.

Perhaps Miffy decided she'd been respectable long enough. She thrust her drink at Max, barked, "Hold this," hiked up her skirt, tore off the stockings and the baggy girdle they were attached to, and chucked the whole doings into the fire.

"Last time I'll ever wear those damn things."

Miffy grabbed the martini back from Max and poured it down her throat. Then she gasped, choked, dropped the empty glass, and doubled over.

For a second, Max was the only one who did anything. He caught the falling body, eased Miffy into a chair, and bent over her trying to make out what was wrong. Then Biff Beaxitt sprang on to his back.

"Get away from her, you murdering devil! First Alice B., and now — "

Now Miffy. She was dead, anybody could see that. Of course Biff was thinking of murder. They all were. How often did a person just drop like that from natural causes? How could it be only coincidence that Alice B. had been killed just three nights ago, right here in Miffy's house, and that her murderer was still at large?

Who knew Alice and her amusing little secrets better than Miffy? Who'd been up and around hunting for Bromo Seltzer when perhaps the blood wasn't yet dry on the axe? Who might be too great a threat to be left alive? And what could have been in that glass, to have worked so horribly fast?

CHAPTER 15

Max had almost managed to wrench free of Biff when Don and Fren Larrington jumped him together. Against the three of them he hadn't a chance. Sarah tried to intervene by shrieking, "Stop it, you idiots," and pounding at them with her fists, but Bradley Rovedock gently pulled her away.

"Don't, Sarah, you'll get hurt. We'd better call the police and let them handle this."

"Oh yes, quickly! Ask for Sergeant Jofferty."

She was sane again, but it was agony to watch Don Larrington ripping off Max's belt and using it to lash his feet together while Biff and Fren tied his hands behind his back. Max caught Sarah's eyes and actually managed a rueful smile.

"Did you send for Jofferty?"

"Shut up, you!"

Fren hauled off to punch Max in the face, but Don struck his fist away.

"Belay that, you damn fool. Next thing we know, he'll be yelling police brutality and getting some left-wing jackass of a judge on his side."

"What do you mean, police brutality? We're not police."

"We're performing a citizens' arrest."

"Like hell you are," said Max. "You're laying yourselves open for a fat lawsuit and don't think I'm not going to win it. Sarah, the car keys are in my right-hand coat pocket."

"Keep away from him, Sarah," bawled Biff. "If you've got any half-baked ideas about rescuing this Jew bastard — "

Sarah was too furious to say more than, "Don, you seem to be the least insane of the three. Would you please reach into Max's pocket and get his keys for me?"

"What do you want them for?"

"I have no other means of transportation. Is that sufficient reason?"

"I suppose so." Don fished out the keys and was about to hand them over when Fren stopped him.

"Wait a minute. How do we know she's not going to rush off and destroy the evidence?"

"What evidence?" Appie Kelling had by now managed to wriggle her way through the press to her niece's side. "I don't understand this at all. I must say it does seem — with dear Alice B. just buried — and now poor Miffy — she — it's hardly — and after all, Mr. Bittersohn is fomally engaged to Sarah. Really, Fren, such roughhousing might possibly be acceptable at the bachelor party, but — "

"Roughhousing, hell! Appie, this man is a killer. First he sneaks in here at night and steals all the paintings and bashes Alice B. with the axe, and now he poisons Miffy's drink. It was a fresh one. She hadn't even touched it!"

One couldn't tell whether Fren thought Miffy's death or the waste of a virgin martini was the worse crime of the two.

"But he's engaged to Sarah," Appie moaned.

"Then Sarah had better get herself disengaged pretty damn fast. This son of a bitch — "

"This man's name is Max Bittersohn," Sarah interrupted, "and I'll thank you to use it, as I myself shall be doing in the very near future."

Fren sneered. "Naturally you've got to say that now. You'll be singing a different

221

tune in a day or so."

"Shut up, Fren," said his brother. "Appie, look at the facts. Mr. Bittersohn," he leaned heavily on the name, "first entered this house, to the best of our knowledge, something like eight hours before Alice B. was killed by a burglar she caught stealing Miffy's paintings. Mr. Bittersohn," again the implied sneer, "is a self-confessed dealer in stolen paintings."

"Correction, Don." That was Bradley Rovedock, back from making his telephone call to the police station. "As I understand it, Bittersohn runs a detective agency that specializes in the recovery of stolen art objects."

"It's the same thing, isn't it?"

"Not quite. I suggest we leave the investigating to the police. They said they'd be right along."

"But darn it, Brad, he handled Miffy's drink. He was holding it while she took her stockings off. We all saw him."

"We did not," Vare contradicted. "We may or may not have all observed Mr. Bittersohn accepting the glass from Miffy's hand, but I should venture to assume that we then focused our eyes on the somewhat unusual spectacle of an elderly woman removing her nether garments in the presence of a large mixed group of guests."

"What's she talking about?" Fren asked Don.

"She means nobody was watching Bittersohn hold the drink because we were more interested in seeing Miffy do her strip tease," Pussy Beaxitt interpreted. "Vare's right, too. I know I was."

"To think that when dear Miffy said this was the last time she'd ever wear — " Aunt Appie started to cry again.

"But that's exactly what she meant," Sarah exclaimed. "Don't you realize how totally out of character it was for her to burn that girdle? You saw what a rag it was. I'll bet it was fifty years old, and she'd hung on to it all this time. Why should she decide to get rid of it right after Alice B. died?"

"Because she was drunk," said Pussy. "Good try, Sarah. You want us to believe Miffy had planned to do a Sarah Bernhardt out of grief over losing Alice B. Forget it. Biff and I rode with her to the funeral and back. She did nothing but bitch the whole way about how she was going to have to hire someone to cook and housekeep because Appie was hopeless and she couldn't stand her flapping around anyway. If that's suicidal mania, I'm Jessica Dragonette."

"Why Jessica Dragonette?" Lassie Larrington wanted to know.

"I don't know, it's just a name that sticks in my mind. My father was crazy about her. We used to listen to her on the radio every Sunday night. It was an Atwater-Kent. I shouldn't be surprised if my mother still has it."

"Why would she keep the radio if this Dragonette woman was your father's mistress?"

"Lassie, for God's sake! She was a soprano on the Bayer Aspirin hour. Father liked to hear her sing. I don't suppose he ever laid eyes on her, much less anything else. Forget I ever mentioned Jessica Dragonette, will you? What I meant was that Miffy did not commit suicide. So if this Bittersohn didn't put the poison in her drink, who did?"

"What makes you so sure Miffy was in fact poisoned?" asked Vare quite sensibly.

"Because she was roaring around in great form, until she gulped down that drink and keeled over. How else could she have died that suddenly?"

"She might have had a massive coronary attack."

"Vare, knock it off," snarled Biff Beaxitt.

"You're supposed to have brains, aren't you? Of course Miffy was poisoned. We've caught the bastard who did it and if Sarah chooses to take umbrage at my use of the word 'bastard,' that's just too damned bad. What I'm wondering right now is who gets Miffy's money."

"You can hardly be intimating that she's left it to Sarah."

"One never knows. If Appie'd been working on her — "

Biff stopped. Even he must have realized he was talking nonsense. Appie Kelling would be the last person in the world to try such a thing, and the first to louse it up if she ever did. Nevertheless, his question had set everybody thinking. With Alice B. gone and none of the Tergoyne family left alive, at least none that anybody knew about, any member of the group Miffy had dominated for so long might stand a fighting chance of getting something out of her estate.

Or if she'd left it all to Alice B. as they'd expected her to, would Alice's heirs automatically become Miffy's residuary legatees? Was that why Tigger's eyes were glittering so from under all that hair, and why Biff Beaxitt had been so quick to dub Max Bittersohn the scapegoat?

Biff himself had been right there in the crowd beside Max while Miffy did her striptease act. So had Pussy. In fact, she'd been about as close to Max as a woman could get unless they'd happened to be participating in a group orgy. Either of the Beaxitts could have poisoned the drink easily enough while the rest were watching Miffy.

But so could any number of other people. Sarah shut her eyes and tried to re-stage the scene in her mind. There'd been Fren and Don and — no, Lassie had been standing over here by the window with Sarah herself. But then she'd made that fuss about her drink and gone to get another. She'd have had to pass near Miffy then, because Miffy hadn't strayed far from the source of supply ever since they'd got back from the funeral.

It might even have been Lassie who'd brought Miffy that fresh drink. Sarah remembered she'd taken two from the bar. Sarah had assumed she'd meant them both for herself, to make up for the tomato juice. It would have been natural enough for Lassie to offer one to Miffy, though, and most unlike Miffy to turn it down. Fren claimed Miffy's glass had been full, and that meant she'd only just got a fresh one. No drink would have stayed untasted in Miffy's hand for long.

But Sarah hadn't actually seen Lassie give the extra drink to Miffy or anyone else. She was still at her mental exercises, trying to recall who'd been standing behind Miffy, when the police arrived. Chief Wilson was among them, but to her regret, Sergeant Jofferty wasn't. At least Wilson and his men appeared competent and not too impressed by Biff Beaxitt's insistence that he'd caught Isaac Bittersohn's boy red-handed bumping off his hostess.

One of the men went off to phone for more help while the chief asked people sensible questions and got mostly irrelevant answers, except from Tigger who still wouldn't do anything but glower. Nobody could swear to seeing Max put the alleged poison in Miffy's drink. Nobody had been conscious of seeing much of anything except Miffy exposing her wrinkled brown hide and hurling a frayed-out elastic girdle into the fire, then drinking from the glass Max had been holding for her, choking, and dying. Nobody could say where Miffy had got the drink in the first place, especially the harried bartender.

"I kept mixin' an' they kept grabbin',"

was his testimony. "I never seen nothin' like it, not even at the Policemen's Ball."

He'd been preparing batch after batch of martinis, since nobody seemed to want anything else. People would hold out their empty glasses for refills, or else he'd pour the mixture into clean glasses and set them on a tray. Either the waitress would pass the tray around or else guests would come over and pick up the drinks, often two and three at a time, and give the extras to their friends.

"You took two, Lassie," said Sarah.

"Yes, and so did a lot of other people," snapped Biff Beaxitt. "Lassie gave her extra one to me, and I drank it. You needn't think you're going to get him off that way, Sarah."

Biff had not taken that drink from Lassie. Sarah wasn't sure how she knew he was lying, but he was. Nevertheless, every single member of the club would back him up. Even Aunt Appie and Bradley Rovedock were giving her sorrowful "How could you let down the side?" looks. She'd queered herself with the old crowd now for fair, and she hadn't helped Max by doing it.

"Then does anybody else know where Miss Tergoyne got that last drink?" Chief Wilson asked.

Nobody could or would say. The bartender was pretty sure Miffy'd got at least a couple for herself from the bar. Bradley Rovedock volunteered that he'd fetched one for Miffy early on but he was sure she'd had several after that. Aunt Appie sniffled that she'd tried without success to persuade Miffy to drink a nice, nourishing glass of tomato juice. After that, they all clammed up.

A little while later, some homicide people who must have been from the state police showed up, along with the medical examiner. He refused to give any definite opinion as to the cause of death until he'd done an autopsy, but muttered to the police that they'd better do a damned careful job of gathering the evidence.

"He thinks it's murder, too," everyone whispered to everyone else. When a fingerprint expert impounded the glass and asked them to line up and have their fingerprints taken, they were sure.

Don Larrington snorted, "Damn bureaucratic balderdash," but he and the rest cooperated readily enough; except for Tigger who had to be threatened with arrest for assaulting an officer before she'd allow her fingers to be inked. Vare looked perturbed at that, as well she might.

Max had been released from his improvised restraints and allowed to put his belt back on. He was sitting quietly in one of Miffy's armchairs, not missing any of the goings-on. Sarah made a move toward him, but one of the policemen edged in front of her. Max himself gave her a warning look and shook his head. After that she stayed put and tried not to panic.

At last the guests were told they could leave. Most were out before the police chief had finished telling them they could go, but the Larrington brothers were still truculent.

"What's going to happen to Bittersohn? You're not letting him go?" asked Don.

"Mr. Bittersohn is going to assist us in our investigation," Wilson assured him.

"What's that supposed to mean?" Fren demanded.

"It's what they have to say before they make the formal arrest." Don, at any rate, seemed satisfied. "Come on, Fren. We told them at the boatyard we'd be there by one o'clock and it's past two already. They'll be charging you an extra day's dockage."

"Oh Jesus!"

Fren followed his brother without further argument. Miffy's body was taken away on a stretcher covered with a blanket. The caterers had collected their belongings and left with the rest. Now only Chief Wilson and some of the other police personnel were left, along with Sarah, Max, Appie Kelling, Bradley Rovedock, and strangely enough, Vare and Tigger.

Appie was trying to get a grip on herself and be helpful. "Sarah dear, don't you think you ought to go home and lie down for a while? Shall I come with you?"

"No, you mustn't leave here, Aunt Appie. Miffy would have wanted you to stay and look after the house."

Sarah neither knew nor cared what Miffy would have wanted. All she knew was what she herself wanted, and it most emphatically wasn't Aunt Appie's help.

"Maybe Vare will stay with the boys for a while," she suggested. "Then Lionel can come up here and keep you company."

Vare shook her head. "I have cast off the shackles of motherhood."

"Right on!"

Those were the first words Sarah had ever heard Tigger say. Tigger jerked her head toward the doorway and Vare followed her out.

"Damn shame their own mothers didn't cast off the shackles before those two bimbos were hatched," observed one of Wilson's men. "Max, what's the scoop here, anyway?"

"That's a hell of a question to ask the chief suspect," Bittersohn replied. "All I can say is, I wish I could tell you."

"Who doesn't?" grunted Wilson. "From what I can gather, almost anybody in the crowd could have poisoned Miss Tergoyne's drink if anybody did, which we don't know yet. I suppose maybe we should have had everyone searched, but what good would it have done? None of them would have been dumb enough to pour out a slug and then hang on to the poison, would they? What I'd do myself, I'd have the stuff ready in a little vial or an eyedropper, something I could palm. Maybe even a plastic bag or a kid's balloon. Just put your hand over the glass, drop in the poison, and throw the container into the fire. If anybody happened to smell something burning, they'd think it was the elastic out of that girdle she burned. Perfect setup."

"With the possible exception that the alleged poisoner wouldn't have known in advance Miss Tergoyne was going to burn her girdle," Bradley Rovedock observed drily. "She didn't, as a rule."

Wilson didn't think that was very important. "They'd know she was going to have a drink, though?"

"Oh yes," said Bradley. "One could be sure Miss Tergoyne was going to have a drink. And no doubt one could have slipped something into her glass easily enough. I could have poisoned her myself, I suppose, if it came to that. So could almost any of the others. The only person I can definitely rule out is Sarah here. That is, Mrs. Alexander Kelling."

"How so?"

"Mrs. Kelling was standing apart from the group, chatting with Mrs. Donald Larrington, if my memory serves me. We'd been sailing together yesterday, though I don't suppose that's relevant. Anyway, Mrs. Larrington came over to the bar after a while and got a drink — or drinks, according to testimony — then came and stood near Miss Tergoyne with the rest of us. Mrs. Kelling stayed where she was. Moreover, she was drinking tomato juice whereas Miss Tergoyne had a martini, as you know. There could be no question of her switching glasses or anything of that sort even if she'd been near enough to do so, which she wasn't."

"Mrs. Kelling never came over to the bar at all?"

"No, she had only that one glass of tomato juice, which I personally handed to her shortly after we'd got back from the funeral. I noticed because I happened to be standing where I could look directly over at her and was wondering whether I shouldn't go over and get her a refill."

"You were acting as host?"

"I suppose you might say so, more or less. One does what one can at a time like that, you know. Appie — Mrs. Samuel Kelling — and I were trying to help hold the fort. With her companion gone, Miss Tergoyne was quite alone in the world, except for her friends."

"You and Mrs. Samuel Kelling were Miss Tergoyne's closest friends, would you say?"

"Not at all. We were simply the two available for the job. Mrs. Kelling is the soul of kindness and I'm," Bradley shrugged, "an unattached bachelor with nothing more pressing to do. In point of fact, neither of us saw much of Miss Tergoyne as a rule. Mrs. Kelling lives in Cambridge and doesn't get out to Ireson's as often as we'd like. I do maintain a house here, as you know, but I'm off cruising much of the time. Still, we'd both known Miss Tergoyne more or less forever and when she asked us for help, we couldn't turn her down. By the way, Appie, I'm quite willing to stay here with you, unless Sarah would like me to — "

He was being much kinder than Sarah deserved, but she didn't even bother to answer him. She turned to Chief Wilson.

"What's going to happen to Max?"

Before Wilson could reply, Bradley laid a comforting hand on her shoulder.

"Sarah, you mustn't worry. It's just an unfortunate coincidence that Mr. Bittersohn happens to have a certain type of expertise and that nothing ever happened until — that is, that he — oh God, how can one put it? He was in the wrong place at the wrong times, that's all."

CHAPTER 16

And it was Sarah Kelling's fault, for having taken up with the wrong sort of man. That was what Bradley was trying so hard not to say. Poor, innocent little Sarah didn't know any better. Did he expect her to be grateful? Nevertheless, he was right and she'd better say so.

"That's true, Chief Wilson. Max didn't know any of these people. He's here mainly because I needed transportation. The other day, before Alice B. died, we'd just got to Ireson's when Miffy called up and said Appie was on her way out by train and we were to come for drinks that same afternoon. I asked Max to drive us over because I have no car of my own just now."

"Sold the old Studebaker, I hear?"

"That's right. Ira Rivkin found someone who promised to give it a good home. What

I'm getting at is that neither of us expected to be at Miffy's that day. This tale of Fren Larrington's about Max casing the joint and planning a robbery is nonsense. Pussy Beaxitt jammed him into a corner and started pumping him the minute he set foot inside this door. Max never got to see anything here except Pussy's big mouth."

"Can you confirm that, Mr. Rovedock?"

Bradley smiled a little. "I can't say I'd have expressed it quite that way myself, but I shouldn't be surprised. As it happened, I got here rather late myself and didn't have a chance to speak to either Sarah or her friend before they left. I do recall that Pussy — Mrs. William Beaxitt, that is — was talking to Bittersohn when I came in. Then Alice Beaxitt greeted him by name and said she'd known him as a boy or something of the sort."

Bradley, how could you? Sarah gritted her teeth.

"Alice B. didn't say she knew him, Bradley. She said she knew who he was. Alice B. always recognized people. She was that sort of person. What matters is that Max had never been inside Miffy's house before, and whoever robbed the place must have known it pretty well. Better than I did, anyway. That list of stolen articles contained any number of things I'd never been aware Miffy owned."

"When did you see that list, Mrs. Kelling?"

Sarah blinked. Maybe Sergeant Jofferty shouldn't have been showing it.

"One of your men was asking Max's professional opinion about some of the items," she replied cautiously.

Wilson grunted. "Oh yeah. Walt Jofferty's quite a pal of yours, isn't he?"

"I'd be proud to think so. Nobody could have been kinder when — " she wasn't going to talk about that any more. "What I'm getting at, Chief Wilson, is that it's absolutely ridiculous to accuse Max just because he happens to know a Fantin-Latour from a Norman Rockwell. Aside from the fact that he's not the sort to go around burgling houses and slaughtering elderly women, he had no time to get organized."

"How long would it take to organize a poisoned cocktail?"

"Quite a while, I should think. Miffy didn't get sick or anything, she just gulped it down and fell like a rock. Most people don't have instantly lethal poisons loose in their pockets, do they? You'd have to find out what to use, get hold of it somehow, then have it ready in some easily manageable form. You said so yourself, remember? And you'd have to be awfully careful how you went about it, or you'd wind up killing yourself, too."

"Okay, that's a point. What else?"

"Well, Max and I almost didn't come to the funeral at all. That is, I more or less meant to come but I'd thought of calling Bradley or someone to pick me up. If I had, I'd have been too late. Lassie Larrington had told me yesterday it started at eleven. As it happened, though, Aunt Appie called while we were having breakfast and said it was set for ten."

"Do you remember what time you called your niece, Mrs. Kelling?"

Appie said she thought it might be around a quarter to nine, or maybe nine o'clock. Or possibly a little later.

"It was half-past, Aunt Appie, because Max and I barely had time to make ourselves presentable and get to the church."

"And you were just having breakfast?"

"Yes. We'd been — well, I'd had Mr. Lomax at the house with his nephew talking about what I wanted them to do today, and then Max came up from the carriage house and we decided to get married so that's why we were late with breakfast."

"I see." Chief Wilson looked amused, then suddenly wary. "How come you decided to get married all of a sudden?"

"Well, it wasn't all of a sudden," Sarah admitted. "That is to say, Max has been asking me off and on for the past two months and I knew I was going to say yes but somehow it was never the right time. This morning it was. We were going to slip away right after the funeral and get the license, but poor Aunt Appie was so upset and her son couldn't come on account of the children and you've seen for yourselves how helpful her daughter-in-law was being, so we stuck around. And look where it got us," she finished bitterly.

The police chief wasn't interested in Sarah's feelings. "You say you had to hurry and get ready for the funeral after your aunt called. What exactly did you do?"

"Went upstairs and changed from pants and jersey into the clothes I'm wearing now."

"Did Bittersohn go with you?"

"No, he did not."

Without realizing what she was doing, Sarah gave an excellent imitation of her

Great-aunt Emma squashing a cheeky up-start. Then she turned pale. Couldn't she have had sense enough to say yes?

"Why don't you let me answer for my-self?" Max was demanding angrily. "I went back to the carriage house, where I'm stay-ing, and put on this jacket and tie. Then I brought the car around to pick up Sarah. I was alone and can't produce any witness to testify I didn't stuff my pockets full of strychnine or whatever the hell it was be-fore I got back to her."

"He does have plenty of witnesses as to what he did once we got here though," cried Sarah. "None of that bunch had the gall to claim they'd actually seen him put-ting anything in Miffy's drink, did they? And you can believe they would have if they could. He was constantly surrounded by a crowd giving him the third degree. Bradley Rovedock can testify to that."

"Third degree may be pitching it a bit strong," Bradley demurred. "Naturally in a close-knit group like ours, any outsider," he caught himself but not quite soon enough, "that is to say, any newcomer becomes a center of interest. People were trying to make him feel welcome."

"I suppose Biff Beaxitt and the Larringtons were trying to make Max feel welcome when they knocked him down and tied his hands and feet? Why don't you arrest them, Chief Wilson? Biff in particular would make a far likelier candidate than Max."

"Why, Mrs. Kelling?"

"Because in case you've forgotten, the woman whose funeral we'd just been at was also named Beaxitt. She was Biff's aunt."

"Cousin, dear," Appie corrected. "Her father and Biff's were brothers. There was quite an age span between them. You wouldn't think it because Biff is so large and dear Alice B. was so petite. Oh, to think we'll never — "

"Yes, Aunt Appie. Anyway, I think both Alice B.'s and Miffy's wills ought to be investigated before anybody jumps to any more conclusions."

"Really, Sarah," Bradley Rovedock sounded shocked. "Biff would never — "

"That's the sort of thing I used to think, Bradley. Under enough pressure, I think Biff Beaxitt might do almost anything. I'm positive Fren Larrington would, after the way he brained that poor goat yesterday."

"Sarah, the goat was injured. Its throat was badly torn."

"He could have made some effort to find

out how badly, couldn't he? We could have cut it loose from that wire and brought it across to the vet."

"And sunk *Perdita* in the process, perhaps? Sarah dear, that was a wild animal, not a domestic pet. Fren did the humane thing. I must say I myself rather admired him for being able to act so quickly and decisively."

"Would you two mind telling me what you're talking about?" Wilson asked, reasonably enough.

They explained more or less in chorus. Sarah's version differed a good deal from Bradley's. It was easy enough to decide which of them the police were more inclined to credit.

"Too damn many goats on Little Nibble anyhow," appeared to be the consensus. As to Fren's executing the beast without a trial, hell, what was a man to do?

Chief Wilson prowled around a little longer, asked a few more questions, then shut his notebook. "Looks as if we've done about all we can do here for the time being. Now Max, just for the record, I guess we'd better go take a look around your place. You're staying with Mrs. Kelling, you said."

"In the carriage house," Appie felt called upon to remind the chief. "It's quite suitable. Normally I'd have been staying with Sarah at the main house. In fact I did stay there the first night. But the next morning we found out — this dreadful thing — and Miffy asked me to — but my son Lionel and the four boys were coming to camp out at Sarah's, so I thought — but then there was that business about the boathouse which I'm not quite clear — but it's all perfectly suitable," she finished gamely.

"Of course, Mrs. Kelling. This is just police routine, you understand. Have to make sure we've touched all the bases, in case somebody starts asking questions later."

"To be sure. It wouldn't be cricket not to touch all the bases, would it?"

Not knowing whether or not that was meant for a joke, Wilson gave Appie an uncertain smile. "You say you were with your niece the night Miss Beaxitt was murdered. You slept well, I hope?"

"The bed was most comfortable," Appie replied primly.

"Yes, but how did you sleep?"

"As well as anyone might reasonably expect to in a strange place. Not that Ireson's is strange, because I'd stayed there so often — but it had been quite a while, you know, because Samuel had been so — and when one is used to nursing an invalid, the least little sound — one does tend to hop up and run, you know."

"Then you passed a restless night."

"Not restless. I rested beautifully, I assure you. It's just that I haven't yet broken the habit — and once one is awake — not every time, of course, but — "

"So you got up. How many times, would you say?"

"Three, I believe."

"And what did you do?"

"My dear sir, what does one do when one gets up in the night? At least when one gets to be my age? I visited the convenience, naturally."

"You didn't happen to meet your niece on any of these — ah — visits?"

"No, although I did peek in to make sure I hadn't disturbed her."

"All three times?"

"It wasn't that I meant to invade your privacy, Sarah dear. It was only because I was so used to checking on poor, dear Sam. And it was comforting to see somebody when I looked. So many times since he died, I've — from force of habit — and there would be the empty bed. One couldn't help — and you did look so sweet, dear, cuddled up like a little field mouse in its nest of thistledown. It is thistledown they use, isn't it? One always likes to picture them that way. So cozy."

Chief Wilson appeared to have no information on the sleeping habits of field mice. "Then what you're saying is that to the best of your knowledge, your niece slept in her own bed all night long?"

"I believe I can state it quite positively," said Appie. "She hardly stirred. I'm sure I didn't hear the bedsprings creak more than six or seven times. Worn out, poor lamb. Though actually we'd spent a quiet enough evening and I'd fixed a nice tuna casserole so she didn't have to — we did have a pleasant time, didn't we, Bradley?"

"I did at any rate," Bradley assured her.

"You were with the Kelling ladies, Mr. Rovedock?"

"Yes, until about half-past nine. Appie — that is, Mrs. Samuel Kelling — had stayed on here after Sarah and Mr. Bittersohn left. When the party broke up, I offered Mrs. Kelling a ride home, and she kindly invited me to take potluck with her and Sarah."

"Where was Mr. Bittersohn when you got there, do you know?"

"Oh yes, we found him sitting by the fire in the living room with Sarah. We all had a drink together, then he said he had to be going, and went."

"Where to?"

"Chief Wilson, this was the first time in my life I'd ever met the man," Bradley expostulated. "I hardly felt well enough acquainted to question him about his engagements."

"Speaking of engagements, were you aware that he and Mrs. Sarah Kelling were seriously considering marriage?"

"Not then, no. As a matter of fact, he was introduced to me as her tenant."

"That so?" Wilson fished out his notebook and opened it again.

"According to the testimony of both Mrs. Larrington and Mrs. Beaxitt, the conversation which took place at the party held here prior to Miss Alice Beaxitt's death between her and Mr. Bittersohn had to do with his love affair with a young woman named Barbara. Would you know anything about that?"

"There was some discussion, I believe, after Sarah and Mr. Bittersohn had left the party." Bradley didn't exactly curl his lip in disdain, but he gave the impression of having done so. "I wasn't paying much attention."

"Oh, but Sarah hadn't known anything about this Barbara," cried Appie. "Not until Alice B. blurted it right out in front of everybody. Poor Alice B. was always so forthright. It never occurred to her — "

"Alice B. was a vicious gossip, and she told the story deliberately to make trouble between Max and me."

Sarah knew better than to tell lies to the police, after the experiences she'd had with them. "She succeeded, if you want to know. Max and I had a big fight about it on the way home. We'd gotten ourselves straightened out and everything would have been fine if you and Bradley hadn't come — " she'd almost said barging in.

"In view of what had gone on, Max didn't feel like hanging around making polite conversation, so he went over to his sister's house and played cribbage with his uncle," she finished.

"But you didn't know where he was going, dear. You'd expected him to stay for dinner, and you asked if you should leave him something. Bradley, you remember."

"Aunt Appie, if you're trying to give me an alibi, forget it. I don't need one. As for Max, his own family can vouch for where he was."

"Neither of you happened to hear him come back?" said Wilson.

"No, but we wouldn't, you see," Appie took it upon herself to answer. "As I told you, he was staying down at the carriage house. It's a fair distance from the main house because of the old days when the horses would — well, I'm sure I don't have to — and the driveway has a turnoff down that way so if he didn't choose to drive up to the main house, which of course he wouldn't if he got back late — "

"Thank you, Mrs. Kelling. Come on, Bittersohn. You can tell us the rest of it in the cruiser."

"What about you, Sarah?" asked Bradley. "Shall I take you home?"

"No, stay here with Aunt Appie. I've got to drive Max's car back. We can't leave it standing here."

"Are you sure you can manage by yourself?"

"Why not? After the Studebaker, I should be able to manage anything."

She gave Rovedock a confident smile and

went out flipping the car keys between her fingers. Once behind the wheel, though, she didn't feel quite so sure of herself. Max loved his car the way a cowboy is alleged to love his horse. Cracking it up on him after what he'd already been put through would be the ultimate blow.

Sarah managed well enough by driving more cautiously than she normally would have. The upshot was that by the time she got there, the police were already hard at work inside the carriage house. When she went in to see what was happening, she saw one of the men had found a loose riser she'd never suspected in the stairway, and was holding it up like the flap of an envelope. His partner had a flashlight and was peering into the cavity.

"Hey, Chief, come here quick!"

Sarah went, too. What they'd found were a small watercolor whose characteristic purple shadows told her at once it was a Millard Sheets, and a long-handled axe that had been almost but not quite wiped clean.

"Sorry, Bittersohn," said Chief Wilson. "I guess we'll have to take you on down to the station."

CHAPTER 17

"You can't blame Max for that," Sarah cried. "He wasn't the one who hid it."

"Then who was?" Wilson asked her.

"I don't know, but I heard it happening."

"Oh yeah? When was this?"

"Last night. Around midnight, I should think. It wasn't too long before Max got back from New York anyway, because I was still in a flap when he came in. I was hunting around the stalls to see if I could find anything wrong. Wasn't I, Max?"

"You were, not that they're going to believe either one of us."

"Let her tell her story," said Wilson. "Go on, Mrs. Kelling. How long did you spend hunting?"

"Perhaps fifteen minutes. After Max came in, we — got sidetracked."

"About this noise you say you heard,

251

where were you at the time?"

"Upstairs in the apartment."

"That so? Your aunt gave me the impression you'd been staying at the main house."

Sarah knew she was the color of a Paul's Scarlet, but this was no time to play coy. "What my aunt told you is perfectly true. It just happened that I'd been down at the campground talking to my Cousin Lionel."

"That's the guy who burned down your boathouse a couple of days ago?" said one of Wilson's men.

"I don't think Lionel himself had anything to do with that. His sons claim they didn't, either, for what that's worth. Anyway, I thought they'd gone but it turned out they hadn't. I'm telling this backward. What happened was that yesterday I went out to Little Nibble with Bradley Rovedock and the Larringtons, as you know. That was when Fren Larrington killed the goat. When we got back about six, the rest went on to dinner somewhere, but I asked them to let me off at my house. I was tired and lay down to rest. I fell asleep. I woke about eight o'clock and wasn't sleepy any more, so I went for a walk. I came across Lionel and his gang down in the clearing where the boathouse used to be, so I stopped to visit with them for a while."

"Visit with them?" said Wilson. "Jed Lomax told me you'd thrown them off your property."

"I had, but they weren't listening. Anyway, they'd come back and built a well-sweep and a lean-to and a firepit. They'd really been working awfully hard. It was getting dark by then, so I didn't have the heart to throw them out again. Lionel and I sat down on a log and he started telling me his troubles. Vare — that's his wife, whom you met back at Miffy's — "

"The one who's cast off the shackles of motherhood?"

"Yes. She's stuck him with the children, who are absolute fiends, I grant you, but that's as much Vare's doing as Lionel's. She's demanding a huge allowance which she shares with her friend Tigger, and being utterly beastly in general. Vare was a Beaxitt, by the way. I'm throwing that in for what should be very obvious reasons. Lionel and I have never been what you'd call close, but he needed somebody to talk to and I had nothing better to do, so I stayed and listened."

"Until when?"

"Oh, tennish, I should think. It had been

dark for quite a while by the time I started back."

"How could you see?"

"I'd brought a flashlight with me. I still wasn't sleepy, so I went down to the beach and walked there for a while, then I came back up to the carriage house to see whether Max was back yet. He wasn't, so I decided to wait for him in the apartment."

"Any special reason?"

"Yes. It was while I was walking on the beach that I'd made up my mind to go ahead and marry him. So I wanted to tell him."

"Nice timing," muttered one of the officers.

"I can't help it, that's what happened. Not that it's really anyone's business but Max's and mine."

"All right, Mrs. Kelling," said Wilson. "So you went upstairs to the apartment. How did you get in? Was the door unlocked?"

"No. That is, the carriage house — where we are now — was, but the upstairs wasn't. I had a duplicate key on the ring with my own door keys, so I was able to let myself in."

"You go prepared, don't you?"

"I've been trained to. My late husband had a thing about it. We're so isolated out here, you see. Anyway, I left the outer door unlocked because I knew Max would be coming in, but I'm sure I locked the door to the upstairs apartment when I went in. I remember being glad I had when I heard the noise downstairs."

"Can you describe that noise, Mrs. Kelling?"

"Scrabbly, I suppose one might say. I thought at first it might be an animal of some sort, then I realized it was a person trying to be quiet."

"You didn't open the door and yell down to see who it was?"

"Chief Wilson, we'd just had a particularly gruesome murder which appears to have been the result of Alice Beaxitt's surprising an intruder. No, I did not open the door and yell down. I kept as still as I could and hoped to goodness whoever was down there wouldn't take a notion to come up."

"For how long?"

"Five or ten minutes, I suppose. It seemed like an eternity."

"How come they didn't see the light in the upstairs apartment?"

"Because I hadn't put one on. I'd had my flashlight when I went in, you see. I don't know why I didn't switch on a lamp, I just didn't. As things turned out, I must say I was awfully glad I hadn't."

"You'd been sitting up there alone in the dark for some time, then, before you heard this scrabbling noise, as you describe it."

"No, as a matter of fact, I'd stretched out on Max's bed and fallen asleep again." That was as close as she needed to get to the truth. "I expect it was the noise that waked me."

"What made you so sure it wasn't Bittersohn coming in that you heard?"

"Because Max always charges upstairs like my Great-uncle Nathan at San Juan Hill. He's been one of my tenants in Boston since January, in case you hadn't realized. I'm quite familiar with the kind of racket he makes around a house. Anyway, it's absurd to think he'd have been sneaking in to hide those things so long after the robbery, and then gone out and made a separate entrance later on. He had no way of knowing I was upstairs."

"We don't know if this noise you say you heard had anything to do with the evidence you found, Mrs. Kelling," said Wilson.

"As for the painting, he might have taken it to New York to sell and not been able to find a buyer, so he brought it back again and put it in the hiding place," suggested one of the other men not unintelligently.

Wilson nodded. "Getting back to this noise, Mrs. Kelling. How long did it last?"

"Not long, unless of course it had been going on while I was asleep. Anyway, I only heard it for a short while, then I thought I heard the outer door creak and a little rattling of gravel on the drive, as if someone had gone. As I mentioned, I lay still for a while longer. Then it occurred to me that what I'd heard might have been one of my cousin's children setting another fire, so I pulled myself together and came down. That's what I was doing when Max came in, sniffing around for any sign of smoke or the ticking of a time bomb or whatever."

"Time bomb? Are you kidding?"

"You don't know those little innocents. There's nothing I'd put past them."

"What about murder?"

"Well, perhaps they'd draw the line at that. I don't believe they knew anything about Alice B.'s at any rate, until they heard me telling their father about it the morning after it happened, because they started shrieking, 'We want to see the body.' "

"They weren't at the funeral, right?"

"No. Lionel asked me whether he should take them and I vetoed it as hard as I possibly could because I knew they'd have turned it into a three-ring circus. For a wonder, he took my advice."

"You say his wife was related to this Alice B., as you call her?"

"Yes, Vare was a niece. From what I was told at Miffy's today, she's been hanging around a good deal of late, apparently trying to get Alice B. to leave her some money. Vare knows all about axes because she's done one of those survival courses. She's going to be in a financial mess if Lionel really cuts off her allowance as he claims he's going to, because Tigger appears to be not only a professional freeloader but a pretty tough character. Vare has no money of her own that I know of, and her parents certainly won't give her any to support Tigger with. I know them. I do think you ought to check out those wills before you do anything else, Chief Wilson."

"Thanks for the suggestion, Mrs. Kelling. As it happens, we managed to think of that ourselves. Miss Beaxitt left her entire estate, which amounts to a little over three hundred thousand dollars, to Margaret Tergoyne. The residuary legatee would have been Alexander Kelling."

"Alexander Kelling?" Sarah stammered. "But — but which Alexander Kelling? That's a common name in our family. I have a cousin Alexander Brooks Kelling, and another — "

"This was Alexander Archibald Douglas Kelling. Got many of those?"

Sarah shook her head. She honestly thought she was going to faint. "None now. That was my husband. Why in heaven's name would Alice B. leave her money to him?"

"The will said 'in memory of our beautiful relationship.' That mean anything to you?"

"Yes." Her voice was shaking. "It means she wanted everyone to believe she'd been Alexander's mistress. If that isn't typical! Alice B. couldn't even get herself murdered without being nasty about it."

"You didn't know about this bequest?"

"Know about it? Of course I didn't know about it. Of all the slimy, rotten — I'm sorry. What's the use of ranting and raving? She's had her fun and I'm left with the consequences. You might as well arrest me, Chief Wilson, because I probably would have murdered that scheming old bitch if I'd known what she was up to."

"Then you don't think there's any chance she might in fact have had some kind of relationship with your husband — back when they were young, I mean."

"You're a brave man to ask me that, Chief Wilson. No, I do not. My husband had been so deeply traumatized, if that's the word, by his one disastrous love affair when he was still practically a boy that he didn't even care to think about sex, much less engage in it with a woman who went around telling everything she knew and a great deal she didn't. It's entirely possible Alice B. did have some kind of romantic crush on Alexander, because he was a remarkably handsome man, as you know. Since he was always courteous and considerate toward everyone, Alice B. may have read more into his behavior toward her than he'd meant to convey. It's far more likely, however, that she was just being funny in her own vicious little way. There's going to be a grand free-for-all among the Beaxitts now."

"What about yourself, Mrs. Kelling?"

"What about me? I have nothing to do with it."

"You were your husband's sole legatee, weren't you? Now that they're both gone, I should think if you got yourself a smart lawyer — "

"I shall certainly do no such thing. Anyway, Miffy lived long enough to inherit, thank God, so I doubt if I'd have any sort of case, assuming I'd ever have touched a penny in the first place. The Beaxitts must be having fits. Three hundred thousand dollars is quite a sum. Oh my," Sarah had been visited by a stray thought. "I wonder if that's why Fren Larrington's started paying attention to me."

"What do you mean?"

"Well, he's recently been divorced as you may know. I shouldn't have put it past Alice B. to start dropping him hints that Sarah Kelling wasn't going to be left so hard-up as people thought. I'm sure they all know to a penny how much I got from my father, which is no great fortune by today's standards, so Fren would have been led to believe I had money coming to me from somewhere else."

"Why would Miss Beaxitt do a thing like that?"

"Partly for fun, partly because she was out to break up Max and me."

"Sarah," Max began warningly.

"Max, you can't be in more trouble than you are already, and I'm not telling Chief Wilson anything he can't find out elsewhere, if he doesn't already know. Miffy Tergoyne was rich, bored, not particularly bright and not at all amiable. Alice B. was her court jester. Miffy liked scandals so Alice B. nosed them out for her. If she couldn't find one, she'd stir up a sensation to keep things lively."

"So you think this Beaxitt woman was trying to break up your marriage to Bittersohn in order to hand Miss Tergoyne a laugh?"

"There'd be more to it than that, of course. Miffy was also a snob of the first water, and one doesn't go around cutting down other people unless one's afraid of them."

"Why would she be afraid of Bittersohn?"

"Because my marrying him would be one more step toward breaking up the old gang. Miffy clung to the yacht club crowd, I suppose, because it was the only family she had left. She'd have liked to see everything go on forever the way it used to be back when she was young and life was one grand party. That was impossible, of course. People grew up and moved away, or joined other clubs, or lost their money and couldn't keep up their memberships. The ones who've hung around are mostly of her own generation and needless to say, they've been dying off."

"But what about their sons and daughters?"

"They haven't the time or don't want to be bothered. I certainly didn't, but I was more or less dragged into it. My late mother-in-law and her husband used to sail out of the club. After he died, she dropped her membership but Miffy kept right on regarding her as one of the group. She liked being included. My husband and I had to tag along because his mother needed somebody with her."

Sarah shrugged. "When I came back this summer, I had no intention of getting involved again, but Miffy was on the phone before I'd fairly set foot inside the door, demanding that I bring Max along so she could get a look at him. She'd already prodded my aunt into coming, to make it harder for me to refuse. I'm sure she and Alice B.

had carefully staged that bit of business about Max's old girl friend, knowing it would embarrass us both and hoping it would start a fight, which it did."

Wilson grinned. "You really had it in for those two, didn't you?"

"I'd have been happy to leave them alone if they'd done the same for me. All I'm trying to do is show you the sort of people they were. You mustn't think for a moment Max and I were their only targets."

"So what you're saying is that any number of people might have had reason to want them out of the way, aside from the money."

"I'm saying you shouldn't be so quick to arrest Max, because it's perfectly obvious he's being set up to take the blame for what somebody else did."

And it was perfectly obvious Chief Wilson was thinking Sarah Kelling would have said the same thing if he'd caught Max Bittersohn with the axe in his hands and a corpse at his feet. All she'd accomplish was to brand herself as another spiteful gossip. He was already moving toward the cruiser, taking Max with him. They didn't even get to kiss good-bye.

CHAPTER 18

Six months ago, Sarah might have gone back to the house, curled up on the sofa, and had a good cry. She was tougher now, and she still had Max's car keys. Ten minutes later, she was at the Rivkins'.

Miriam was in the kitchen alone, stirring a potful of boiling macaroni shells. "Hi, Sarah, just in time for a cup of tea. Why so glum? Isn't Max with you?"

"No, he's been taken to the police station. Miriam, where's your uncle, quick?"

"Mike drove him downtown to buy a *Wall Street Journal*."

"How long ago?"

"Just before I started the macaroni. I'm making *kasha varnishkes*. Fifteen minutes maybe. They ought to be back any time now, unless they stop for — you said Max is at the police station? Look, maybe I'd

265

better call Freddy's."

Miriam ran to the wall phone and dialed the one shop in Ireson Town where it was possible to buy both a *Wall Street Journal* and a halfway respectable cigar.

"Freddy, this is Mrs. Rivkin. Are my son and my uncle there? They are? Then tell them to cut it short and get back here fast. The house is on fire."

She hung up, giggling weakly. "Oh my God, what did I say that for? Freddy's calling the fire station right now, I'll bet. Sarah, sit down before you fall down. Eat something."

Sarah was going to say, "I couldn't," then she realized she hadn't had a bite since breakfast except that glass of tomato juice at Miffy's. Maybe if she got some food inside her, she wouldn't feel so wobbly. When Miriam slid a cup of hot tea and a chopped liver sandwich in front of her, she took a bite. Then she remembered Max hadn't gotten any lunch either, and pushed the plate away.

Miriam was eyeing her anxiously. "You don't like chopped liver?"

"It's not that. It's — oh, Miriam!"

She mustn't start bawling. There was no time for that now. She must keep her head and explain exactly what had happened. What she in fact said was, "Max and I are going to get married."

"Mazel tov! How soon?"

"I don't know," Sarah took a sip of the hot tea to steady herself. "That's the problem. I have to get him out of jail first."

"What do you mean, jail? What's he done?"

"Nothing, that's just the point. Somebody's trying to make it look as if he did the robbery and killed Alice B. and Miffy."

"Miffy who? What are you talking about?"

Sarah told her, stammering, choking on the food she was trying to force down, wiping at her eyes with a paper napkin when she couldn't be brave any longer. Miriam went on stirring the macaroni, her face grim and her jaw set.

"And so — that's it." Sarah tried to take another nibble at her sandwich. "I'm sorry, Miriam. It's very good, but I just can't eat."

"You're crazy about him, aren't you?"

"Oh yes."

Miriam took the macaroni over to the sink and drained it, turning her eyes away from the steam. Then she came and sat down across the table from Sarah, heavily, like the middle-aged woman she suddenly was.

"I knew it was going to be you, that very first night when he went to the gas station looking for you after your first husband was — " she shook her head. "My kid brother. God, what's Ma going to say?"

"I know what she's going to say, Miriam. She's going to say what they're all saying about me down at the yacht club. Why couldn't he have stuck with his own kind? But we are the same kind. Miriam, I didn't go chasing after your brother. I've given him every excuse to get out of my life if he'd wanted to go. Right now I'm ready to do anything that might reconcile your parents to our getting married, but I can't give him up to please them or anybody else. Why are we even talking about it? It's too late for talk. Where's your uncle, for heaven's sake?"

"Take it easy, Sarah. They just drove into the yard."

Mike burst into the room before his mother had got the words out of her mouth. "Where's the fire?"

"There isn't one," Miriam told him. "Your Uncle Max has been arrested and we need Uncle Jake to get him out. I wasn't going to explain all that to Freddy, was I?"

"Oh Ma! You and your inhibitions. Uncle Max has got pinched before. What's he in for this time?"

"They're trying to claim he killed those two women from the yacht club and stole all their paintings."

"No kidding!" Even Mike was impressed by that one. "It's a frame."

"Of course it is," said Sarah. "That's what I've been trying to tell Chief Wilson, but he won't listen. Uncle Jake, you've got to get him out."

"So?" said the older man. "Uncle Jake, is it?"

"Sarah and Max just got engaged," Miriam explained wearily.

"Nice timing. You said two women. Who's the second?"

"Miffy Tergoyne," Sarah told him. "The one who owned the paintings. Max had driven me to Alice B.'s funeral — that's the one who got axed to death at the time of the robbery. We weren't going back to the house afterward but we did on account of my Aunt Appie. Miffy gave Max her drink to hold while she was taking off her girdle. Then she took the glass back from him and drank what was in it and fell over dead."

"Wait a minute. How come she took off her girdle in front of Max?"

"It wasn't just Max, it was in front of everybody."

"That's how they act over there?" Miriam gasped.

Sarah felt a twinge of anger. There it was again, the they-and-we thing, even from the woman who was going to be her sister. And how often had the Rivkins been invited to join the yacht club, and how many black-balls would they have got if they'd ever tried?

"No, that's not how they do it," Sarah told her. "That's what Miffy happened to do on this particular occasion. She was an elderly woman who'd been through a dread-ful experience, she was probably still in shock, she'd had far too much to drink, and she's always been a little bit batty anyway. I'm so used to her that it didn't even strike me as a strange thing for her to do. She'd worn the girdle to hold up her stockings. As a rule she never wore stockings at all, summer or winter. I suppose they were bothering her."

"So how come she gave the glass to Max?"

"Because he happened to be standing right in front of her. Can't we please go get him now?"

"Out of where?" asked Jacob Bittersohn. "Have they lugged him off to the county jail, or what?"

"I don't know. They said they were going down to the station. You see, they'd found the bloodstained axe and one of the stolen paintings hidden in the carriage house where Max is staying. I tried to explain, but Chief Wilson thought I was only trying to cover up for Max."

"Look, could we start from the beginning?"

Under the lawyer's expert questioning, Sarah managed to tell a coherent story. When she'd finished, he nodded.

"So they detained him for questioning. Come on, let's go post bail."

"Will they let us?"

"Don't worry, they'll be glad to get rid of him. All it takes is money."

"Then I'd better get hold of Cousin Dolph first. He has scads of money. He hates to part with any, but his wife will make him. Mary adores Max."

"We're not exactly paupers ourselves," Bittersohn said rather huffily. "Let's find out how much they want before we push the panic button. Who wants to come to the bailout?"

"Me," said Mike. "How about you, Ma?"

"No, go ahead without me. I've got to call your grandmother before, God forbid, she hears it from somebody else."

"Please reassure her it's all a stupid mistake," Sarah begged. "The police will have to clear him of any suspicion soon."

"The police?" Miriam shrugged. "That's Uncle Jake's department. It's the engagement I'm worried about."

CHAPTER 19

"They got the medical examiner's report while I was there."

Max spoke wearily. The bailing-out had taken too long. He was sitting in the back seat of his own car, perhaps for the first time since he'd bought it, with both arms locked tight around Sarah.

"That cocktail must have been about half gin and half nicotine. It's a wonder the woman lived long enough to swallow it."

Mike answered him without turning his head. He was driving the car, Proudly but somewhat nervously. "Must have tasted gruesome."

"That wouldn't have mattered to Miffy." Sarah's voice sounded muffled because she was burrowed against Max's chest. "She'd drink anything if it came in a cocktail glass. But how could the poisoner have dared?

Max, what if you'd got the glasses mixed and drunk it yourself?"

"I wasn't having anything. Therefore it looks as if the object of the exercise was in fact to get rid of Miss Tergoyne and have me take the rap for it. I wish I knew whether making me the fall guy was just a matter of convenience or something personal."

"Any rabid anti-Semites in that crowd, Sarah?" Uncle Jake asked sharply.

"I honestly don't know, Uncle Jake. Some of them aren't above making disparaging remarks about Jews and I'm sure Max and I shan't be invited to join the club, but I daresay if we or you were to ask them out to an expensive restaurant, they'd graciously permit us to pick up the check. They're not all like that, of course. I'm talking about real dimwits like the Beaxitts and the Larringtons. Miffy herself was the worst of the lot, but she'd hardly have poisoned herself to throw the blame on Max just because he's Jewish."

"If she'd been pickling her brains in straight gin all those years, who's to say what she might be crazy enough to do?"

"I did think of suicide," Sarah admitted. "Lassie Larrington was with Miffy in the funeral car, though, and she claims all Miffy did was fuss about having to find a new housekeeper because Alice B. used to do the work. She didn't act depressed when she was talking to you, did she, Max?"

"She acted sloshed. Or did she always undress in public?"

"She might have if she'd taken the notion, but she'd never burned her clothes before. Miffy was always so tenacious of her possessions that Alice B. claimed she used to have to sneak the garbage out when Miffy wasn't looking. Actually that was what made me wonder about suicide. Remember how she said 'I'll never wear this again,' and chucked that old girdle on the fire just before she took the drink?"

"Maybe she killed herself on a sudden impulse," Mike suggested.

"How could she? I don't know anything about nicotine except that people used to put it on plants to kill bugs instead of that stuff in the squirt cans they have now. Maybe they still do, but it hardly seems like stuff one would leave lying around the living room. Furthermore, Max would have seen her fussing around with the bottle or whatever it came out of. Miffy couldn't do anything without making a big to-do about it."

"What about this drink?" said Uncle Jake. "Who poured it for her?"

"They had a guy there tending bar," Max told him, "and a couple of women passing things. As far as I can remember, one of the waitresses brought over a trayful of drinks and Miss Tergoyne took one."

"It wasn't the last one on the tray?"

"I don't think so. About fourteen people were grabbing at once. I'm inclined to rule out the possibility that the drink was poisoned while it was still on the tray, unless whoever had the nicotine didn't give a damn who drank it. You know, if it hadn't been the Tergoyne woman herself who got killed, I'd say she might have staged her strip act for the purpose of attracting everyone's attention and giving an accomplice the chance to poison the drink I was holding."

"Could that have been done without your noticing?"

"Why not? Hell, I was gawking with the rest of them. If someone had the stuff palmed, as Chief Wilson suggested, it wouldn't take you a second to slop in a slug. If any happened to drip on my hand, I'd have thought I was spilling her drink, that's all. Or somebody was spilling one on me. You know how it is, you put fifty people in a room big enough to hold an army and the next thing you know, forty-seven of them are clustered together in one tight little knot. It's the herd instinct."

"So you herded?"

"Uncle Jake, I was what they were herding around. Miss Tergoyne was pumping me about my sex life, and the rest were trying to hear what I said."

"What did you say?"

Sarah giggled. "Max is pulling your leg, Uncle Jake. Miffy could be awfully rude, though, and I must say I'd never seen her quite so dreadful as she was today. Of course before this she'd always had Alice B. to handle the grilling. Alice was somewhat less blatant and a good deal more clever about extracting information. She'd have made a good Gestapo agent, I always thought. Pussy Beaxitt's no slouch, either. She was right there panting to get at you, but Miffy never gave her a chance. You know Max, that idea of yours about Miffy's cooking up some scheme that backfired might be something to work on. Maybe she thought if she handed you a martini you'd automatically start to drink it. She would."

"But if there'd been poison put into it, why would she drink it herself after I handed it back to her?"

"Reflex action, maybe."

"Horsefeathers, my love. All she'd have to do would be to spill it accidentally and get another."

"Hey," Mike called over his shoulder. "I hate to interrupt this interesting discussion, but where are we supposed to be going?"

"You'd better drop me off before you go home," Sarah told him. "I think Miriam's seen as much of me as she cares to."

"What's that supposed to mean?" Max demanded.

"What would you expect? Miriam feels that if it hadn't been for me you'd never have got into this situation and she's absolutely right. I'm sure your uncle is thinking the same thing, only he's too polite to say so."

"No I'm not," said Jacob Bittersohn. "I know damn well it's not your fault. I also know if Maxie weren't in this schemozzle, he'd be in another. You think this is the first time I've had to bail him out? Look, Miriam will understand. Ira will understand. Isaac will understand. As for my sister-in-law Bayla — oi! You happen to have a spare bedroom at your place?"

"Five, and you're welcome to them all," Sarah told him.

"That's good," said Mike, "because if Uncle Jake has to fly the coop, I'm coming with him. Hey, what's this?"

He'd started swinging into Sarah's drive, only to be confronted by a barricade of sawhorses, a huge "No Trepassing" sign, and a vigilante with a well-sharpened scythe.

"Mr. Lomax," Sarah gasped. "What's this for?"

"To keep people out." The self-appointed sentry brought his scythe to ground-rest.

"What people, for goodness' sake?"

"Ev'rybody an' his brother, just about."

"But why? Oh, good heavens! I suppose it's been on the news about that axe turning up in the carriage house?"

"Manner o' speakin'. That lowdown nephew o' mine," Lomax bent his head so low that the long beak of his cap hid his entire face. "I'm ashamed to own 'im," he muttered.

"What's he done? Gone around telling his friends we've had the police up here?"

"Worse'n that."

Lomax straightened up and faced them as squarely as another Jed Lomax had faced the Redcoats at Bunker Hill. "Pete's been runnin' around with a strumpet that works for the caterin' service. After the caterer finished at Miss Tergoyne's, Pete snuck off to help eat up the leavin's. She told 'im what happened over there, so the pair of 'em hightailed it back here. They was spyin' through the bushes when Wilson an' his boys was searchin' the carriage house. They seen the axe an' the pitcher, an' they seen Max gettin' carted off in the cruiser. They decided they could rake a buck on it, so they started callin' the newspapers an' teevee stations."

"Then that is the absolute last time — " Sarah began, but Mr. Lomax held up his hand.

"You needn't tell me to fire Pete, 'cause I already done it. I'd o' fired myself for bein' fool enough to trust 'im in the first place, only I figured somebody'd better stay an' hold the fort till you got back here or there'd be nothin' left o' the place."

"Mr. Lomax, you must never dream of quitting. Whatever would I do without you? Name me one family that doesn't have a rotten apple on the tree. I'm just grateful you were around and had the presence of mind to block off the drive. I'd better get out here and walk up."

"The hell you will," said Max. "We're

sticking together. Mike, hop out and move those sawhorses, will you? Jed, you know my nephew Mike, Ira's son? And this is my Uncle Jake."

"Known Mike since he was knee-high to a gas pump."

Lomax shifted his scythe to the left hand and struck his right through the open car window. "You must be Isaac's brother the lawyer. Pleased to meet you, sir. You been down gettin' Max off the hook in time for the weddin', I s'pose."

"Mr. Lomax," cried Sarah, "how did you know that? Don't tell me Pete — "

"Nobody told me nothin'. I got eyes in my head, ain't I? Tarnation! Here comes another o' them mobile camera units. You folks hightail it on up to the house. I'll stay here an' stave 'em off."

"I'll help," said Mike. "Got a tire iron, Max?"

"No bodily assault," his great-uncle warned him.

"Don't worry, Uncle Jake. I know all about lawsuits. I'll just hurl myself in front of the truck and let them run over me. Then Ma and Pa can sue the television station instead."

"A *goldene kind*. Move it, Maxie."

Max had taken his usual place at the wheel. He gunned the big car up the drive, out of sight of the cameras.

"A good man, Lomax," Jake commented, "but what can he do just guarding the driveway? Can't they sneak in across the fields?"

"Not unless they want to get torn apart," Sarah told him. "We've allowed brambles to grow up around the edges of the property for years, in order to keep trespassers out and provide shelter for wildlife. By now they're twenty feet high and forty feet thick. On the beach side there's a high, sandy cliff that's next to impossible to climb except by the stairs. We'll have to think of some way to guard those. Max, turn down the boathouse path, will you? If Lionel and the boy bandits are still around, a spot of guerilla warfare ought to be right up their alley."

CHAPTER 20

"Lionel," said Sarah, "you do have the most magnificent sense of timing."

Who else would have got the bright notion of repairing the collapsed boathouse jetty at precisely the hour when letting any outsider land here could set off the ultimate calamity? Worse yet, Lionel and his crew had made a first-rate job of it.

"Thank you, Sarah." As usual, Lionel was disgustingly pleased with himself.

"As you observe, we are employing the selfsame principle of sled and rollers that was doubtless used to move the blocks of stone for the pyramids of Egypt, the megaliths of Stonehenge, and other so-called wonders of the world. The boys scoured the beach and the woods for boulders of suitable size while I busied myself constructing a ramp and cutting poles to

283

serve as rollers. These poles will later become part of the raft we plan to build tomorrow. We had hoped to construct a canoe according to the precepts set down by Henry Wadsworth Longfellow in his epic poem *Hiawatha*, but your woods appear to be sadly lacking in paper birches, not to mention the fibrous roots of the tamarack, or larch tree."

"Lionel," said Sarah, "forget the larch trees. We're under siege."

"I beg your pardon?"

"You see those two motorboats out there?"

"Certainly I see them. They appear to be headed this way. Splendid. Now we shall be able to test the efficacy of our reconstruction."

"Lionel, if you let those boats land, I'll slaughter you."

"Sarah, are you quite well?"

"I'm livid. We've got a television unit trying to get up the drive and God knows what's happening at the cliff stairs. I'd thought this area was safe from invasion because the jetty'd fallen down and blocked the cove; now I find it's the most vulnerable spot of all. Lionel, I will not have any outsider on this property. You will not allow anybody — not excluding your pals from the yacht club, your wife, or most particularly her girl friend — to set foot on that jetty without official permission from either myself or the police. Do you understand?"

"Sarah, you exhibit symptoms of paranoia."

"I'll exhibit symptoms of homicide if you don't keep them off. Lionel, you owe me this."

"But why?"

"Because the axe that killed Alice B. has been found in our carriage house and the reporters are going crazy."

"Wow! Let's see it."

The boys, who'd been distracted from their rock-hounding by their elders' talk, gathered around and began to clamor.

"Shut up, all of you," Sarah shouted. "No, you can't see the axe. It's at the police station and that's where you'll be, Woody, if I catch you peddling tickets to sightseers. Jesse and James, get in the car with Mr. Bittersohn. We need you to guard the cliff stairs. The rest of you stand by here to repel boarders."

"You might have explained sooner," Lionel fussed. "To provide ourselves with ordnance is hardly feasible at this juncture. Had I known in time, I could have constructed a simple *ballista*, or at least a *catapulta*."

"I didn't know myself until two minutes ago. Can't you just yell and throw rocks at the boats?"

"Pikes, that's it! Equip yourselves, lads."

Sarah left her cousin issuing pointed staves to Woody and little Frank, who was prattling in childish glee about what fun it would be to run somebody through the guts. Max drove the other two to the top of the cliff and gave them their orders.

"Stay right here and don't budge. If anybody tries to come up, yell your heads off."

"How about if we roll down boulders on top of 'em?" James offered helpfully.

"Don't you dare. You could kill somebody that way."

"I know," cried Sarah. "Fish heads."

"What?" said Max.

"Come with me."

She grabbed a shovel and a couple of Alexander's fire-fighting buckets out of the carriage house and ran down to the compost heap where excess orts from the fish factory simmered and reeked in the June sun.

"Shoo, gulls." She scared off a gaggle of

feeding birds, and started filling her pails.

"My God," gasped Max from behind his handkerchief. "That stuff stinks to high heaven."

"I know. A glob of secondhand entrails straight in the face ought to discourage almost anybody, wouldn't you think? Here, carry this pailful up to the boys, quick. Don't get it near your clothes."

"Sarah, I've had a rough day."

Nevertheless, Max picked up the noisome load and lugged it back up over the knoll. Craven that he was, he sent Jesse back for the second bucket. Unlike Max, Jesse was all enthusiasm.

"Neat-oh! How about if we plaster this stuff all over the stairs? That'll draw the sea gulls and they can bomb the bad guys."

"Good thinking. If you run out, there's plenty more right here. Just don't both leave the stairs at the same time. Have fun."

Molly Pitcher might have handled the situation with more finesse, but Sarah had done the best she could. She handed over the shovel to Jesse, and went to take a bath. When she came downstairs, showered and changed, she found Max having a rough time on the telephone.

"Too bad you feel that way, Ma. Maybe you'll change your mind when you meet her."

He hung up so gently that it was clear he'd much rather have ripped the phone out of the wall. Sarah went over and put her arms around him.

"Max, I'm sorry."

"She'll get over it. And if she doesn't, what the hell?"

He rubbed his face against her hair. "How about a glass of tea for me and Uncle Jake?"

"You poor love, I'll bet you never got a bite of lunch."

"They gave me some lousy coffee and a stale doughnut down at the station."

"Police brutality! I'll fix you a sandwich right this minute. Would your uncle like a whiskey?"

"Let's skip the booze, if you don't mind. I'm feeling sort of teetotal."

"I don't wonder. Just a second till I put the kettle on."

While the water was heating, Sarah put together some chicken sandwiches and cut slices from a particularly luscious dark chocolate cake that had been one of Cousin Theonia's contributions. When she carried the tray into the living room, she found Max and his uncle sprawled in two dilapidated easy chairs before the fireplace, which held only gray ashes and a few crumpled papers. She threw on some driftwood and touched a match.

"To make the room a bit more cheerful," she remarked. "How do you take your tea, Mr. Bittersohn?"

"Mr. Bittersohn, all of a sudden. How come no Uncle Jake? You mad at me?"

"No, but I'm not sure how you feel about me."

"Neither am I. Lemon and two sugars, if you've got it."

Jake Bittersohn took a sandwich, chewed appraisingly, then leaned back stirring the tea Sarah gave him. "So where are we? Max?"

"Please let him alone till he's had his tea," Sarah begged. "You know, I'm wondering about that woman friend of Pete Lomax who works for the caterer."

"What's to wonder?"

"For one thing, I wonder whether it was her idea or his to call the papers. I'm inclined to think it was Pete's, because if any woman who's trailing around with a man like him isn't a tramp she must be an idiot.

In my personal opinion, Pete Lomax is no good."

"And how much is your opinion worth? I'm just asking." Jake helped himself to another sandwich as a gesture of goodwill.

"Enough to get by on, I think. I do run a boarding house, and I've had a fairly wide experience of human nature. I've also seen far too much of Pete lately while he's been up here working with his uncle. He's sneaky, he's lazy, he's nasty-minded, and I doubt whether he'd stick at a spot of violence. He almost slaughtered one of my cousin's boys the other day, as Max can tell you."

Max nodded with his mouth full.

"Ever since I heard about the robbery at Miffy Tergoyne's," Sarah went on, "I've been thinking there must have been two people involved, one inside who knew what to take, and one outside to collect the stuff and pack it into their getaway car."

"So?"

"So Pete must know that house pretty well. He and his uncle were doing odd jobs for Miffy during the off-months when there weren't any of the other summer people around. Miffy always thought she got the work done cheaper then."

"Which she didn't."

"Of course not. Mr. Lomax would simply quote her a high price and then let her beat him down to what he'd normally charge."

"Now you know why a Jew could never make a living off a Yankee," Jake Bittersohn remarked to his nephew. "So all right, everybody's happy, nobody takes a beating, what's that to do with the robbery?"

"Nothing except that Pete, being there with his uncle, would no doubt have seen Miffy and Alice B. going around with the book."

"What book?"

"Miffy had this inventory album with photographs and descriptions of her more valuable pieces. I've never seen it myself, but my Aunt Appie has. She stayed with Miffy for several days once when Alice B. was having her appendix out, and she said Miffy went through the entire house every single morning, checking things off in the book to make sure they were all present and accounted for. I've also heard her friends joking about it, though never in front of Miffy."

"Then in fact anybody who got hold of this inventory book could have pulled off the robbery that the police are insisting had to be done by an art expert."

"Anybody who knew the book existed

and had wits enough to use it, certainly."

"Then how come the police are so anxious to pin the robbery on Max?"

"I don't think they are. I think they're being pressured by the yacht club crowd. All they have to go on is that Miffy insisted she'd slept with the book under her pillow and that it couldn't have been taken away without waking her, which is absurd. She'd drunk herself into a stupor as usual and wouldn't have cracked an eyelid if somebody'd stolen the bed from under her."

"Could you swear in court that she had in fact been dead drunk the night of the robbery?"

"No, of course I couldn't. Nobody could have, I don't suppose, except Alice B., and she's dead."

"Any chance this Alice B. and your guy Pete robbed the house together, and that he killed her after she'd handed the valuables out to him?"

"Good heavens, I never thought of that."

Sarah thought of it now, then shook her head. "It would be easy enough, at any rate. But why should Alice B. steal from Miffy? She got everything she wanted from Miffy as it was, and she stood to inherit the whole estate when Miffy died."

"How do you know?"

"Everybody knew. At least we all assumed — "

"Don't give me assumed. Who's Miss Tergoyne's lawyer?"

"Mr. Pertwee here in town, as far as I know. At least he acted for her in a couple of lawsuits. She was always after somebody about something."

"Pertwee, eh? I know him. Good man. Where's your phone?"

"In the front hall."

"Excuse me."

Jacob Bittersohn set down his empty cup and left the room. Sarah mended the fire and took out the tea tray. Max dozed. After a while the lawyer came back, looking pleased with himself.

"Margaret Tergoyne did not and apparently never intended to leave her companion a nickel. The existing and presumably valid will executed about fifteen years ago divides Miss Tergoyne's estate equally among Pauline Larrington Beaxitt, Laura Beaxitt Larrington, and Appolonia Kelling Kelling. Know them?"

"Pussy, Lassie, and Aunt Appie? I can't believe it."

"Believe it."

Sarah shook her head. "I'm — dumbfounded. Of course Miffy knew Alice B. had money of her own, and perhaps she considered that since she'd supported Alice all those years — but still — is there any way Alice B. could have found out?"

"How big is Pertwee's office?"

"Not big at all, I shouldn't think. I've never been inside, but I know it's in his house and his wife does most of the secretarial work. Mrs. Lomax used to go in and help out once or twice a week until her arthritis got so bad she had to quit. I don't know whether they've got anyone else to replace her."

"Mrs. Lomax, eh? Would that be your caretaker's wife?"

"Yes."

"How does she get along with the nephew?"

"I have no idea. I can't imagine her telling tales outside the office, if that's what you mean. She's not that kind of woman."

"How well do you know Mrs. Lomax?"

Sarah pondered that one for a moment, then had to confess, "Not well at all, really. The Lomaxes tend to be somewhat feudal about not trying to be on social terms with their employers. I've stopped there with messages a few times and she rides up here with her husband in the truck once in a while when he isn't intending to stay long. We pass the time of day, I ask about her arthritis, she makes some polite comment about the lilac bushes or whatever, and that's the extent of our conversation. Mrs. Lomax has always impressed me as being an intelligent, well-bred, self-respecting woman. More than that, I can't honestly say."

The lawyer nodded. He had the most beautiful head of thick, wavy, iron-gray hair Sarah had ever seen on an older man. Max's would be like that in thirty years. Right now Max was sound asleep in the easy chair, with his head wobbling around and his mouth slightly open. She must indeed be far gone to find him so totally adorable in such an absurd posture.

"Tell me about Alice Beaxitt," the elder Bittersohn commanded while Sarah was tucking a sofa pillow behind Max's neck

That was easier. Sarah told him all she could think of, including the dirty trick Alice B. had played on Max at the party.

He pushed out his lower lip and thought about it for a while. Then he said, "Interesting. If this Tergoyne woman was such a dumb soak and the companion so clever at minding everybody's business, it doesn't add up. How could Miss Tergoyne keep her will a secret for so long, and why should Miss Beaxitt stick around doing the work if she wasn't going to get anything out of it?"

"But Alice B. got a great deal out of it," Sarah reminded him. "I've told you Miffy paid the bills. Obviously Alice B. never spent a cent of her own money, otherwise how could she have left so large an estate of her own? That is, assuming the money's really there and the will isn't just another of Alice B.'s little funnies."

"The money's there, according to Pertwee. Okay, so Alice B. is riding the gravy train, she's got a hefty pile of her own stashed away. Would that reconcile her to being left completely out of Miss Tergoyne's will?"

"Maybe not," Sarah admitted. "Alice B. was a vain woman. She was always bidding to be the center of attention in one way or another, and I know she liked having people regard her as Miffy's heiress. She was younger than Miffy by several years and took much better care of herself, so she'd naturally have expected to be the survivor. I think it would have rankled dreadfully if she'd known that some day the truth would come out and she'd face the humiliation of having people know Miffy'd regarded her as something between a paid companion and a charity case. She wouldn't flounce off in a huff because after all, she did have a good thing going at Miffy's, but it wouldn't surprise me if she'd known for years and nursed the grudge until she could think of a way to outwit Miffy and get what she thought was coming to her. Look at how long Alice B. must have remembered that bit of information about Max, and never used it until the moment came when she could make a big effect with it. That's how she was."

Sarah was getting excited about this idea. "As you know, we've had a series of robberies around the summer colony. Suppose Pete Lomax has been doing them and Alice B. found out. She did have an unbelievable sort of underground network. She could blackmail Pete into helping her, not that he'd need much coaxing if he thought he was going to get a share of the profits. Or what if she simply sized Pete up as the sort who'd steal if he got the chance?"

"What if isn't evidence," the lawyer objected.

Max was awake now. "Let her talk, Jake. Go on, Sarah. What if Miss Beaxitt did maneuver Pete into helping her rob Miss Tergoyne? How come they took only works of art? Silver and jewelry would have been easier to fence."

"Yes, but Alice B. wouldn't have been doing it for the money. She didn't need that. What she'd have wanted was to hurt Miffy without risking being caught. That meant she'd need somebody else to pin the crime on. You'd be the perfect somebody because you weren't one of the crowd, yet you were somebody local who knew the lie of the land and had the right sort of expertise."

"She didn't know me," Max objected.

"But she knew about you, didn't she? I shouldn't be surprised if Alice B. had made her plan while you were in the living room and she was out in the kitchen filling her clam puffs. She could have telephoned Pete easily enough from there to make himself available that night. I shouldn't be surprised if they'd even worked up some kind of innocent-sounding code message she could leave with a third party.

"She wouldn't have to make any other preparation except to make sure Miffy had a good stiff nightcap, because she was familiar with the inventory book and knew exactly which pieces an art expert would go for. I expect she deliberately dropped that remark about your old girl friend to send you off in a huff. Then she could claim you came back and robbed the house as an act of vengeance."

"Sounds like a plot from Verdi."

"I know, but Alice B. was like that, all theatrics and offstage noises."

"So she axed herself to make the plot more convincing?" Jake grunted.

"Oh no, Pete would have thought of that for himself. He'd know he'd never be safe from that tongue of hers as long as Alice B. was alive, and he is a violent man. She'd have been easy to kill because an attack on herself would be the last thing she was expecting. Alice B. was always the attacker, not the victim, and then it was with words instead of weapons. By doing away with her, Pete would be not only freeing himself of a menace but getting to keep the loot."

"And how was a man like him going to fence a lot of stolen paintings?" Max asked mildly.

"How do I know? If he was involved in previous robberies, he must have connections, mustn't he? Or perhaps Alice B. had lined someone up. She might have cooked up a lie about Miffy's wanting to dispose secretly of some valuables with her acting as the intermediary. She might have got a dealer to believe her, or at least pretend he did, if he thought he could make a good thing out of it."

"It happens," Max agreed.

"Alice B. would have been the one to think of planting the Millard Sheets on you, though Pete must have built that neat little hiding place inside the staircase. He's fairly good with tools."

"Okay," said Uncle Jake, "but how did he manage to kill Miss Tergoyne in a roomful of her friends when he wasn't even there?"

"Easily enough, I should think, if his lady friend was the waitress. Working around these old gardens as Pete does, I should think he could have found nicotine in somebody's potting house or shed. It's supposed to be banned now, I believe, but you know how people leave things poked into corners for years and years.

"As to why he'd want her dead, Miffy's brains weren't so entirely pickled in alcohol that she wouldn't recall Pete's being around the place and maybe taking too much interest in things that were none of his business, like the inventory book. Being Miffy, she'd tackle him straight-on and tell him he'd better get her paintings back fast or she'd blow the whistle on him. She'd be more concerned with retrieving what was hers than with any high-flown humbug about seeing justice done."

"That's not bad," said Max. "She'd have given him a deadline, I suppose. He'd have to shut her up before it came around and he couldn't produce. That's why he'd run the risk of killing her publicly like that, instead of waiting till dark and backing a truck over her. I suppose the waitress could have managed to slip Miss Tergoyne the poisoned drink. She might have kept her hand on it while she was passing the tray to make sure nobody else got that particular glass. She'd be taking an awful chance, though, juggling a deadly poison around like that."

"Maybe she didn't know it was poison. Pete could have told her the nicotine was only some kind of practical joke like knock-out drops or stuff that would make Miffy throw up in front of her company. That's the sort of thing Pete would think was funny. Or if the waitress is the tenderhearted type, Pete could say it was medicine the doctor couldn't get Miffy to take any other way. Anyway, I think it was pretty dim of Chief Wilson not to get hold of that waitress instead of you."

"Here's the man to tell," Max remarked as a familiar face appeared at the side door. "Hi, Jofferty. How'd you get past the sentries?"

"Flashed my clamming permit at 'em. Ol' Jed's roped in five or six of his cronies and they've got quite a cordon down there. He claims Mike's gone up on the cliff to bombard invaders with fish heads. I suppose he knew what he was talking about."

"Oh yes," Sarah told him. "Two of my cousin's boys were already there. I don't know how Mr. Lomax heard about the fish heads, though. That was what you might call an inspiration of the moment."

"Jed always knows. Understand you folks are having another run-in with the law out here. I'm sorry I wasn't on duty when they pinched Max."

"So am I. I did tell Bradley Rovedock to ask for you when he called the station to let them know about Miffy Tergoyne's being killed, but evidently he didn't connect. I'm sure you'd have been able to talk some sense into Chief Wilson."

Sarah felt strange talking to Jofferty in his off-duty uniform of plaid shirt and rubber waders, but she couldn't have been gladder to see him. "Could I offer you something, Sergeant? We've been having tea, but there's whiskey or beer if you'd rather."

"Thanks, but I had coffee at the station just now when I dropped in to get the scoop on Max. The chief's having the time of his life, running up the town's phone bill making sure you were where you said you were yesterday in New York, Max."

"I hope to God he's succeeding."

" 'Fraid so. Looks as if he's got to bait up his lines again and go catch himself another suspect."

"Sarah's got one lined up for him."

Max told him who and why. Jofferty nodded.

"Good thinking, Mrs. Kelling. The only hitch is, on the night Alice Beaxitt was killed, I myself picked Pete up about half-past ten for driving under the influence. We kept him in the lockup till morning. I'm afraid Pete's got what you might call an ironclad alibi."

CHAPTER 21

"Hell!" said the proper Bostonian.

Uncle Jake snickered. Sarah turned red.

"I'm sorry, but it was such a lovely theory. I was even going to add that the Bilbao looking glass got here because Pete brought it. I can't see how we found the thing before the robbery took place, if Alice B. didn't give it to Pete. She was the only one who could have pretended the glass was still there the next morning when she took inventory for Miffy, as I suppose she must have. Assuming there weren't two different glasses involved."

"I snuck a copy of the photograph they had in that album," said Jofferty, "and went over to the bank and compared it to the mirror we found here in your entryway. Took a Polaroid of that one, too, while I was about it. They sure look alike to me.

Were those mirrors all made to the same pattern?"

"No they weren't," Max told him. "Assembly-line production hadn't been invented in those days. Designs followed the same general scheme, but details could vary a good deal. Even if one particular craftsman tried to make a perfectly matched pair, there'd still be subtle differences in the graining of the marble."

He studied the two photographs Jofferty handed him. "I'd say they're identical. You shown these to anybody yet?"

"No, and I'm going to catch hell from the chief because I haven't. I had a hunch I'd better keep my mouth shut until you gave me the word. This must have been part of the scheme to frame you, eh, Max? I suppose they figured they'd better get the mirror into the house before anybody showed up, what with Sarah's aunt coming and all. Sorry, Mrs. Kelling. I didn't mean to — "

"I'd much rather you called me Sarah," she told him. "I shan't be Mrs. Kelling much longer anyway, assuming we can keep Max out of jail long enough to get him to the church."

Jacob Bittersohn's eyes narrowed. "The church?"

"The whatever will make Max's mother feel better. I don't care who performs the ceremony, I just want to keep it simple and get it over. Going back to that looking glass, though, I still say it couldn't possibly have been here when we arrived unless Alice B. had deliberately tricked Miffy into thinking it was still in their house. If Pete Lomax wasn't Alice B.'s accomplice, then somebody else was, that's all."

"Couldn't it have been stolen after they'd done their daily check and before you folks got here?" Jofferty suggested.

"I wondered about that, but it would have taken some awfully clever footwork. Alice and Miffy weren't early risers. It was apt to be almost noontime before Miffy'd recovered from her previous night's hangover enough to see straight, much less do her inventory. And how could the thief know he wouldn't run smack into us? We didn't know when we were coming ourselves, until we got here. We'd meant to be earlier, but things kept coming up, then Max got a phone call from Honolulu. Besides, that would mean stealing the looking glass in broad daylight."

"But if Miss Tergoyne and her companion went grocery shopping for the party — "

"Miffy never went anywhere if she could help it, except down to the yacht club. Alice B. would have done the shopping, either the day before or while Miffy was on the phone rounding people up. Come to think of it, I suppose she could have brought the looking glass herself, if she'd had any way to get into the house. No, she wouldn't have done that because she didn't drive. Miffy wouldn't go to the expense of keeping a car, so they either bummed rides from their friends or used the station taxi. Besides, being in the village as they were, Alice B. could walk to the store and back easily enough. She'd have trotted around on her errands alone and gone back to make her clam puffs."

"While she was plannng a murder?" Jofferty was having a hard time with this.

"Alice B. wouldn't have been planning a murder," Sarah reminded him. "She'd have been planning a robbery and she'd have been feeling pretty cocky about it because she'd think she had a foolproof setup. One doesn't go around suspecting little ladies who make hot clam puffs, does one?"

"Okay, Sarah, I'll hand you the clam puffs. But if she had an accomplice and it wasn't Pete, who's your next candidate?"

"One of the Beaxitts, I suppose, since they were her next of kin. My cousin's wife Vare did come to mind, or rather her girl friend Tigger. She's the woman they practically had to chloroform before she'd let her fingerprints be taken."

"Oh yeah, I heard about that one. They're checking to see if she has a record. And she's a niece or something, right?"

"Vare is, but it appears to be Tigger who's after money. And then there's Lassie Larrington, who's one of Miffy's heiresses. On account of the tomato juice, you know."

"Huh?"

"Oh, I'm sorry. You see, at the funeral, or rather afterward at Miffy's, most of the crowd were clustered around Miffy and Max. I was standing apart trying to think of a way to rescue him and chatting with Lassie. She was complaining about how flat the Bloody Marys were. I told her she must have taken a glass of plain tomato juice, which I myself was drinking. Naturally Lassie threw a fit and rushed over to the bar. She got two martinis. Biff Beaxitt claims she gave one of them to him, but I have the impression he's lying."

"Would he cover up for her in a case of murder?"

"Probably, if he thought it was worth his while. Biff and Lassie are cousins or something, and he's married to a relative of Lassie's husband. She's the Priscilla Beaxitt who's another of Miffy's heirs. He'd be protecting the family name, you see, and also the inheritance. It was really most unlike Lassie to make a mistake about a drink. What if Biff knew she'd used that bit of byplay to bring Miffy a poisoned drink while she was crowding in among the others?"

"Always what if?" moaned Jacob Bittersohn. "How about evidence?"

"How about motive?" said Max. "Are the Larringtons hard up?"

"I don't know. Don was complaining yesterday on the boat about the terrible state of the stock market, if that means anything."

"Would Lassie be up to braining Alice Beaxitt with an axe?"

"I should think so. She's one of those big outdoorsy types, like all the yacht club crowd. It might actually be easier to swing an axe than poke a knife into someone, mightn't it? You wouldn't have to be so particular where you hit, and the axe itself would do more of the work because it's so heavy and sharp."

"Cripes, I hadn't thought of that. I mean, when you think of an axe you automatically think of a man." Jofferty shook his head in chauvinistic wonderment.

"Look at Lizzie Borden," Max offered helpfully.

"Never mind look at Lizzie Borden," snapped his uncle. "Look for evidence that might stand up in court. Go on, Sarah. Anybody else you could make a case against?"

"Fren Larrington would be a likely starter. He's Lassie's brother-in-law. Fren's a stupid lout with a really dreadful temper. He's been divorced not long ago, and there might have been some fairly raw stuff they managed to suppress at the trial. Being the sort of person she was, Alice B. could have got hold of the inside facts and used them to blackmail him into helping her."

"Facts?" said the elder Bittersohn inexorably.

"Well, I suppose there's the fact that Fren's started paying me attention all of a sudden. For instance, he barged in here day before yesterday while Max and I were eating breakfast and ordered me to meet him at the yacht club that night for dinner. Yesterday on Bradley Rovedock's boat, he went

310

through the motions of throwing a snit because I hadn't gone. It wasn't very convincing, but I suppose if he's been planting false evidence here, courting the widow would give him some semblance of an excuse to be hanging around if anybody saw him on the premises."

"Speaking of hanging," said Jake, "how come he'd have hung that Bilbao looking glass you kids keep talking about in plain sight? Is he that stupid?"

"But he didn't," Sarah contradicted. "That is, he did but it wouldn't normally have been, if you follow."

"I don't."

"Then come with me."

She led him into the cramped little front entry. "The glass was hanging here, on this wall. You couldn't help noticing it when you came in the front door, but the point is, we almost never do. The side door into the living room is much more convenient, and that's the one everybody always comes to. It just happened the day Max and I arrived, I had my purse full of junk and the key to this door was the first one I found, so I used it. Otherwise, the looking glass might have hung here for days, maybe even weeks, without my noticing."

"And these Beaxitts and Larringtons would have known that?" Jake was asking as they went back to join Max and Jofferty.

"Alice B. would, at any rate. She knew I never got around to cleaning the entryway because it wasn't used, so she always made a point of coming to the front door. Then we had to race around and find the key."

Jofferty stood up. "I'm beginning to wonder why somebody didn't clobber that Beaxitt woman long ago. 'Fraid I've got to beat it, folks. The wife's expecting me with a bucket of clams for supper. Hey, Sarah, you want some nice steamers?"

"I'd adore just a few. I'm the only one who'll eat them. Here, take this bowl to put them in."

"Okay. It'll take me a minute or two. I left my car down by the road so Jed wouldn't have to move his barricade."

"I'll drive you down," Max offered. "I expect Uncle Jake wants a lift back to Miriam's."

"He's welcome to stay and eat with us," said Sarah.

"Thanks, but if I know Miriam she's been cooking all afternoon and she'll be sore if I don't show up." The older man dragged himself out of the chair he'd just got settled back into. "You want to ride over with us, Sarah?"

"No, I'd better wait for the clams."

Sarah had a feeling she might not be received with open arms at the Rivkins' just now. Besides, she had her own cooking to start. She was out in the kitchen puttering around when she heard, "Yoo-hoo! Anybody home?"

"Aunt Appie!"

Sarah rushed back to the living room. "How did you get here?"

"Pussy and Biff came over to house-sit, so Bradley and I decided we'd play hooky and here we are. Though I must say we had quite a time getting here. What's all that fuss down at the end of the drive? I actually had to speak sharply to Mr. Lomax before he'd let us through."

"Lomax does seem to be taking his responsibilities as caretaker somewhat over-zealously, we thought," Bradley drawled.

"I couldn't agree with you less," Sarah informed him rather crisply. "If it hadn't been for Mr. Lomax, we'd be overrun by television crews and souvenir hunters by now."

"Great Scott, I hadn't realized. One doesn't really expect such things to happen, but we did collect a mob down at Miffy's, come to think of it. Luckily there was a policeman outside moving them on. Your problem is on account of that scoundrel who tricked you into renting him the carriage house apartment, I gather. He's been arrested, they tell us. That must be a load off your mind, at any rate. Pussy had some yarn about the police having found the murder weapon and one of Miffy's paintings hidden among his socks or whatever, but I expect she got it wrong as she so often does. Surely the man wouldn't have been that stupid."

"No, Max is far from stupid," Sarah answered, "and I'm surprised whoever planted that evidence against him thought such a silly trick would work. Pussy was right about the police finding the axe and the painting, but they weren't in Max's apartment. They'd been hidden behind a loose board in the staircase."

"How ingenious," said Aunt Appie. "I knew he was clever. What a pity he was never taught not to go around killing people. I blame the parents, myself. Dear, shall I make you a nice cup of tea?"

"I've just had one, thanks, with Max and his uncle. Would you please try to get it through your head that my fiancé hasn't killed anybody? As for his parents, they're furious with me for getting him in with the wrong crowd."

"Well, dear, I'm afraid that's what happens when people don't stick with their own kind. For a truly happy marriage — "

"Like Lionel and Vare's?"

That wasn't kind and Sarah was sorry she'd said it, but not very. Appie and Bradley exchanged looks.

"Appie, didn't you say you wanted to get some things out of your luggage?" said Bradley.

Perhaps that was a prearranged signal. Appie blinked twice, then took off upstairs like one of the Ganlors' goats bounding over the crags of Little Nibble. Bradley stretched out a hand to Sarah.

"How about pouring us each a drink and sitting down with me for a little chat?"

What could she reply except, "Scotch or sherry?"

"Sherry would be a pleasant change. I'll throw on another log, shall I?"

Sarah would much rather he didn't. A cozy tête-a-tête by the fire could only mean Bradley was about to unload some unwelcome counsel about getting rid of Max Bittersohn and returning to the fold. She'd already heard enough of that from both sides of the fence, but how could one be rude to Bradley Rovedock? She might as well let him say his piece, then say hers and get it over. Sarah took the drink she didn't particularly want and joined him on the sofa.

"How's *Perdita?*" she asked for lack of a more intelligent opener.

"I haven't been aboard since our little cruise."

Bradley stretched his legs toward the fire, and took a sip of his sherry. "I think this is the first happy moment I've spent since that day. You're a restful person to be with, Sarah."

After Aunt Appie, who wouldn't be? Poor Bradley! The penalty for being kind and available must be a dreadful one sometimes. She smiled back at him, and he laid his free hand lightly over hers.

"You don't know how I've envied Alex all these years."

This wasn't what she'd expected. "But why?" Sarah stammered. "Alexander's life was one long deprivation. You've had everything you wanted."

"I haven't had you, Sarah."

Bradley's hand closed tight. "For a long

316

time now, I've been breaking the commandment about coveting my neighbor's wife."

"How can you say that?" she answered in bewilderment. "You hardly knew me as Alexander's wife, compared to the years you'd known me as a kid growing up. Bradley, if you're trying to be gallant, I wish you wouldn't."

"I'm trying to be honest. Dash it, Sarah, do I have to spend the rest of my life being that nice old buffer who used to take you sailing once in a while?"

"There's no reason why we can't — " Sarah faltered. There was every reason in the world why she couldn't expect Bradley Rovedock to invite her on any more of his agreeable day cruises once she'd become Mrs. Max Bittersohn.

Bradley either thought she'd meant something else, or pretended he did. "Of course there isn't, no reason at all. Sarah darling, please listen to me. I can give you the kind of life Alex always wanted you to have, the life you're entitled to by birth and breeding. We'll straighten out that nonsense with the High Street Bank right away and you'll never have to worry about another thing, ever again. God, when I think of your being forced to turn your beautiful old home into

317

a common boarding house!"

"Hardly common, Bradley." What in God's name had she got herself into now? "We run a very deluxe operation, I assure you."

"Now who's being gallant?"

His lips were much too close to her ear. "Sarah, my adorable child, you don't know how much I admire the way you've made the best of a bad situation. Believe me, though, if I'd known about it in time, you wouldn't have had to."

She edged away as best she could without being too obvious about it. "Bradley, I do have relatives of my own who'd have bailed me out if I'd let them. I chose to deal with my own problem in my own way, and I can't say it's done me any harm."

"No harm? Getting mixed up with — Sarah dear, you've been through such a long ordeal, I'm afraid you're not thinking quite straight. What you need is a complete change of scene and a good, long rest. What do you say we two slip quietly aboard *Perdita* and sail off by ourselves? Go poking among the islands up around Casco Bay, perhaps, just to give you a chance to get used to *Perdita* and me. I promise to behave as a perfect gentleman. As long as you want me to."

He was caressing her hair now. This had to be stopped. Sarah stood up.

"Bradley, I'm going to marry Max Bittersohn as soon as we can get a license."

"Bittersohn? That jailbird? Sarah, you're mad! I'm sorry, dear, I didn't mean that. You're bewildered by the terrible things that have happened to you, and Bittersohn's managed to take advantage, God knows how. You should never even have known that sort of person."

"I gather it's all right for me to know an oaf like Fren Larrington."

"Fren at least is one of our own crowd, and he's managed so far to stay out of jail. Sarah, think of Bittersohn's background. That shyster lawyer for an uncle, a brother-in-law who runs a filling station, his father a common laborer — "

"Jacob Bittersohn is hardly a shyster. Ira Rivkin's an agreeable, intelligent man who's built up a good business from nothing at all. As for being a common laborer, I'm one myself. Anyway, Max's father is one of the most respected men around here, as you'd know if you ever bothered to talk to the natives."

"Sarah — "

"Bradley, I don't know what sort of

romantic notion you've built up about me, but honestly you've got it totally wrong. I'm not the person you seem to think I am. We have different sets of values, we don't even like the same kinds of people. There's no sense in going on with this. It would only end in a fight and I don't want that. I'm too fond of you."

"And isn't that enough to go on with? Sarah darling, I'm afraid you're the one who's having romantic notions. You can't throw yourself away like this. Can't you understand what's happened? After Alex died, you were feeling lost and helpless. This Bittersohn came along and got around you somehow, just as he wormed his way into Miffy's house. And I don't have to tell you the consequences of that."

"You certainly don't, because you've obviously got them wrong, too."

"My dear girl, look at the facts. Bittersohn's even had the gall to drag you into this ghastly mess, trying to make you look like his accomplice. The police aren't fools, you know. Don't you think they suspect you of having shown him that hiding place behind the stairs in the carriage house? How else could he have found it? Surely Alex must have told you he and I built that cubbyhole together when we were boys. God, to think of its being used for such a purpose!"

"I never knew about any secret hole in the stairway, Bradley. I expect you and Alexander swore an oath of secrecy when you built it, and he never broke his word. He'd do that, you know."

"Sarah, don't try to shield that fellow. He isn't worth it. Good God, he even had the effrontery to hang Miffy's looking glass right in your front entryway!"

Sergeant Jofferty, holding Sarah's bowl of steamer clams, stepped into the darkening room. "How'd you happen to hear about us finding that Bilbao looking glass, Mr. Rovedock?"

"Who the hell are you?"

Could this be the Bradley Rovedock she'd known all her life? Or had she ever known him? Sarah said what she had to.

"This is Sergeant Jofferty of the Ireson Town police. Tell him how you knew about the looking glass, Bradley."

"Why, I — " Rovedock began to look wary. "I suppose Pussy Beaxitt must have told me, or Lassie Larrington. They're generally the ones who know what's going on. I don't recall, actually. Everybody at the club's been talking about this ghastly affair, of course. That's only natural, isn't it?"

"Did whoever it was tell you how the glass happened to be found?" Jofferty asked him.

"What was there to tell? I assume you just looked and there it was. You can't blame Mrs. Kelling for not having known, Sergeant. She herself never uses the front door, none of the Kellings ever have. Alice B. used to joke about it as a sort of terra incognita."

"Where the spiders grew big as cats and nobody'd swept down the cobwebs for the past seventy-seven years," Sarah finished for him. "Don't you think that ever got back to us? Think hard, Bradley. Who told you about the looking glass?"

"I can't remember, I've already said so. Whatever does it matter?"

"It matters plenty, Mr. Rovedock," Jofferty told him, setting down the bowl of clams and shifting his stance a little. "You see, the police didn't find that looking glass. Sarah and Max found it as soon as they came out here. They called me right away. I came over and took the glass, all wrapped up, to the police vault in the bank, which I'm in charge of. I filed no report.

We agreed among us not to say a word to anybody, and we haven't. The only people who knew where Miss Tergoyne's looking glass could be found were myself, Sarah Kelling, Jed Lomax, Max Bittersohn, and the guy who hung it in her front entry."

"But Bittersohn was the man who hung it there. Can't you see that?"

"No I can't, Mr. Rovedock. Max came out from Boston with Sarah, he'd never been inside Miss Tergoyne's house, he didn't know he was going till they wound up at that cocktail party, and that was after I'd already taken the glass away. Furthermore, it was Max's idea to hide it and keep quiet about it. He knew something so valuable had to be stolen property, and he figured our best chance of catching the thief was to keep our mouths shut and see what happened. Now can you think of anything you'd like to tell me?"

Bradley shook his head. "Sarah never uses that front door."

"I did this time," said Sarah. "Too bad, Bradley, but there it is. My grandmother always did say the Rovedock fortune came from piracy and the opium trade. I should have remembered sooner. All those vaguely described cruises, all those unsolved robberies. Alice B. found out what you were up to, didn't she? And she started black-mailing you to pull one with her. And you knew what would happen if you did, so you had to kill her."

"Sarah, whatever has come over you? You've always been such a docile little thing."

"Not docile, Bradley. Outnumbered. It was blackmail, wasn't it?"

He only looked at her.

"You might as well talk, you know. *Perdita* won't be hard to trace. It will all come out fast enough, now that you've blown your cover."

"Blown my cover?" Bradley let his lips curl in a fastidious sneer. "Is that the sort of talk you've been picking up from Bittersohn?"

"That and a lot of interesting information about running antiques. It's hard for anyone to prove they've been stolen once you've got them out of the country, isn't it? I expect someone with your background and connections wouldn't have much trouble disposing of a cargo."

"Sarah, you did say you were fond of me."

"That was before you started trying to plant your crimes on an innocent man because you thought he was too low in the social scale to matter. You really are a pirate, aren't you, Bradley?"

"If you say so, my dear. Since I appear to have worn out my welcome here for some reason I still don't quite grasp, perhaps I'd better think of taking my leave. Mind if we have one last drink for the road?"

He picked up the sherry bottle and started to pour. Jofferty leaped to pry a tiny glass vial out of his hand.

"No you don't. None of that big suicide scene stuff. Thought you'd poison your own drink for a change, eh?"

"No, Sergeant." For the first time, Bradley Rovedock hoisted the black flag. "Not mine. Sarah's."

CHAPTER 22

Like her son, Appie Kelling had a magnificent sense of mistiming. She chose that particular moment to bustle into the living room, wreathed in smiles.

"Well, my dears, are congratulations in order? Sarah, I'm so happy for you!"

She tried to throw her arms around her niece, but Sarah shoved her away.

"For God's sake, Aunt Appie, not now."

"But why, dear? And whatever is that man doing to dear Bradley? Here, you sir, stop it at once."

Bradley had counted too heavily on the natural superiority of the Rovedocks. He was tough, but Jofferty was a man of the clam flats.

"Sarah, reach in my hip pocket and get out the handcuffs, will you? The wife's always jawing at me about carrying 'em around in my civvies. Claims it tears hell out of the pockets. But like I tell her, you never know when they'll come in handy. Hold still, you bugger. I've got to read you your rights."

Jofferty had completed the formalities, deputized Sarah to phone the chief, and was tying Bradley's feet with Bradley's own elegant silk ascot when Max Bittersohn came back, carrying a plate covered with aluminum foil.

"Miriam sent over some *bubka*. Where's Sarah? Hey, what the hell's going on here?"

"Precisely what I have been endeavoring to ascertain," Appie Kelling replied with unaccustomed hauteur. "Bradley and I had it nicely arranged that he was to marry Sarah and bring her to her senses. Now I find him being manhandled in this coarse and brutal fashion. I presume his assailant is one of your henchmen?"

Sarah came back from telephoning. "He's a policeman and he's arresting Bradley for murder, among other things."

"Oh, but it was Miffy who killed Alice B.," cried Appie. "She told me so herself. I've been wondering whether I ought to tell somebody, but it seemed so callous to blacken her name, now that she's atoned — "

327

"Wait a minute," said Jofferty. "If this lady has a statement to make, she'd better give it to the chief. Is he coming, Sarah?"

"Yes, he said he'd be right over, and he's bringing some men with a cruiser to get Bradley."

"A cruiser?" Appie gasped. "You mean a *police* cruiser? Sarah, I don't understand this at all."

"Aunt Appie," Sarah said in desperation, "why don't you go out to the kitchen and make us a nice cup of tea and some hot buttered toast?"

"Why, dear, if you really want me to — "

"It would be a wonderful help."

That was all Appie needed. She sped kitchenward. "Well," said Jofferty. "I guess we might as well sit down and wait for the wagon, like it says in the song."

"I insist on being allowed to contact my attorney," said Bradley Rovedock.

"You're supposed to wait till you're booked before you have your phone call, but what the heck, if Sarah doesn't mind. Come on and don't try anything funny unless you want a broken arm."

Jofferty untied Bradley's feet, got his handcuffed arms in a neat back lock, and led him out into the hall. Sarah took the opportunity to give Max a quick rundown on what had happened while he was gone.

Max didn't appear surprised. "I'd already put out a few inquiries on Rovedock," he told her. "Any guy who spends that much time cruising and doesn't try to show you any colored slides of where he's been is the sort of guy I automatically start wondering about. You sure know some peculiar people, *kätzele*."

"So Bradley was trying to tell me a little while ago."

She snuggled against him. "Oh well, now that I've been the downfall of Bradley Rovedock, I don't have to worry about being dropped by the yacht club crowd, or what's left of it. I would feel dreadfully about Bradley, I suppose, if he hadn't tried to pin everything on you. And if he hadn't called me docile."

"You, docile!" Max snorted. "I could tell him a few things." He started to refresh his memory, but she shoved his hand away.

"Chief Wilson's here. Do you want me arrested for indecent exposure?"

"See what I mean?"

Reluctantly, Max abandoned his research and went to open the door. Wilson looked happy, as well he might.

"Understand you folks have a present for me."

"We certainly do," Sarah told him. "And Sergeant Jofferty's been absolutely magnificent. He saved my life, for one thing, so please don't be stuffy with him about withholding evidence on the Bilbao looking glass. Max and I talked him into it in the first place."

"Just a second, I'd better start writing this down."

The chief took out his notebook. Jofferty frogmarched his prisoner back into the living room.

"You care to make a statement, Mr. Rovedock?"

"Only that I intend to bring suit for false arrest as soon as this preposterous farce is played out."

Under heavy escort, Rovedock walked calmly out to the waiting police cruiser.

"Wow, he's a cool one," Jofferty commented. "Sarah, where's your aunt gone to? She said she had something to say."

"Just a second, I'll go get her."

Sarah went out to the kitchen and found Appie up to her knees in flour.

"I'm so sorry, dear. There didn't seem to be enough bread to make toast for so many people, so I thought I'd whip up a nice batch of biscuits. Only somehow the flour canister — "

"Never mind that now, Chief Wilson wants to talk to you. Here, let me dust you down a bit so you won't track flour all over the house. Would you mind wiping your shoes on this mat?"

"Of course, dear."

Appie scrubbed with vigor. "There we are, all defloured. Except that my hair must be — "

"Don't worry about it. Abigail Adams powdered hers, so why shouldn't you?"

"Fancy that. I never knew dear Abigail powdered her hair. I thought she simply went gray from having to put up with John."

Sarah didn't argue the matter, having in fact no recollection of whether dear Abigail had or hadn't, but simply ushered her aunt into the living room.

Appie's first words were, "But where is Bradley? Chief Wilson, I wish to lodge a complaint against that man over there."

She pointed to Jofferty. "I myself caught him being physically abusive to our dear friend Bradley Rovedock."

"I'll make a note of it, ma'am," said Wilson. "Now I understand you have something to tell us about Miss Tergoyne murdering her companion, namely Alice Beaxitt. She confessed to you, did she?"

"I don't know that you'd call it a confession, exactly. Not a formal confession, at any rate. To tell you the unvarnished truth, Miffy wasn't quite herself at the time."

Wilson scratched his chin with his pen. "Suppose you just tell me as accurately as possible what Miss Tergoyne said."

"Let me see. Miffy began by rambling on about how Alice B. talked too much. That was what alerted me to the possibility that something was wrong, you know, because as a rule Miffy was always encouraging Alice B. to talk more. Alice B. did have such an amusing way of expressing herself, though I did think sometimes a little more charity — however."

"Why did Miffy, by whom I gather you mean Miss Tergoyne, think her friend was talking too much?"

"Because she said it meant they couldn't trust her."

"Whom did she mean by they?"

Appie hesitated. "Bradley's name did come up, but I'm sure Miffy didn't mean — "

"Mrs. Kelling, it's not our place to decide what Miss Tergoyne meant. I only want to know what she said. If you could recall her exact words — "

"Oh dear, my poor old brain isn't — would it be cricket for me to refresh my memory by listening to the tape first?"

"The tape? Holy cats, you don't mean you recorded this conversation?"

"I assure you there was no impropriety attached. My motive was wholly disinterested and humanitarian. To be quite frank, as I see we must be, poor Miffy had fallen into the habit of imbibing more freely than was good for her. Mind you, I have no objection whatsoever to a congenial drink among friends, but when I saw the amounts of gin Miffy was literally pouring into herself — you see, I'd gone to stay with her after dear Alice B. was so tragically — anyway, I'd come to realize something must be done."

Mrs. Kelling smoothed her skirt, sending up a puff of flour. "You are perhaps not aware that I have considerable experience in medical matters. My husband was an invalid for many years. Naturally, he read copiously — I do mean copiously, don't I, Sarah? — about illnesses and new treatments and all that, and discussed them with me at great length. Not that he suffered from poor Miffy's sad affliction, you understand. My husband was an abstemious man. Just a glass or two of Guinness with his lunch because Guinness is good for you, you know, and a little port after dinner to help him sleep. And a dash of brandy in his eggnog. But I'm digressing, am I not?"

"Well — "

"I know, cut the cackle and get to the hosses, as dear old Sam used to say. Anyway, I remember his telling me about some people who were cured of alcoholism because somebody took moving pictures of them while they were in their cups and showed them the films when they got sober again so they could see how silly they looked. I couldn't take pictures of Miffy, of course, but I did have my tape recorder with me, so I thought perhaps that would do."

"Mind telling us how you happened to have this tape recorder in your possession at the time, Mrs. Kelling?"

"If you promise you won't laugh."

"We wouldn't dream of it," Wilson assured her.

"Here goes, then, and mind you, not a snicker! You see, I live in Cambridge. Our

334

house used to be in a lovely, quiet residential area, but you know what happens in cities. More and more traffic over the years, until one gets so used to the noise one doesn't even hear it until it isn't there any more, if you follow. It's got so that when I come out here to Ireson's, the quiet gets on my nerves and I simply cannot sleep. Naturally that's not something one can complain about to one's hostess, so what I did was to make myself a tape recording of our familiar Cambridge street noises and bring it along. I use the little earplug, so that I shan't bother anyone else, and play my squeaks and honks and backfires until they lull me off to sleep. Works every time."

She beamed at him and added, "I am so sorry about the biscuits."

Wisely, Chief Wilson didn't attempt to make sense of that remark. "But you told me in our previous interview that you'd spent a wakeful night here."

"Well, the tape runs for only half an hour, you see, and one does feel it wouldn't be quite the thing to keep on rewinding it all night long."

"I see. You don't have the tape with you now, by any chance?"

335

"As a matter of fact, I do. Right here in my handbag somewhere. Ah yes, here we are."

She fished around in that mammoth receptacle and pulled out one of the smallish, inexpensive tape recorders. "To tell you the truth, I was a bit dubious about leaving it at Miffy's while Pussy was there. One understands natural curiosity, since one has a goodly share of it one's self, but I should not have liked Pussy to be playing my tape. Since you're in a position of authority, however, voilà!"

Wilson took the small black box, looking a trifle bemused. "So all I have to do is push the button and out comes her confession."

"If you choose to call it one. She rambles, you know. But the part where she talks about hitting Alice B. with the axe — I really should have hated to have Pussy — but I did think someone — so kind of you to take the responsibility off my shoulders. Oh dear, I never did make the tea, did I?"

"Never mind the tea," said Wilson. "Cripes, Bittersohn, I wish your uncle were here. Would a judge let us introduce something like this as evidence? Surreptitious taping — "

"It was hardly surreptitious," Appie interrupted somewhat angrily. "Surely you don't think I'd — what is that silly word? — bug Miffy's bedroom? I explained to her quite clearly what I was doing, and why."

Chief Wilson put his finger on the "play" button. A wild shrilling of sirens emerged.

"Oh, that's the traffic noises. You'll have to turn the tape over. I only had the one with me, you see, so I used the other side. Be sure to flip the rewind switch first so that you can hear me, too. I'm at the very beginning."

Wilson fumbled for a second or two, then Appie Kelling's voice came on, sounding pompous and tinny.

"Now, Miffy, let me explain that I've turned on my tape recorder because I want you to hear what sort of nonsense you're talking. I am doing this for therapeutic purposes, with the intention of helping you to reduce your excessive consumption of alcoholic beverages."

"God, you bleat like a sheep."

The voice was slurred but unmistakably Miffy's. "Think I give a damn what you do? Needn't get any ideas about moving in here, sponging on me the way Alice did. Gave her every damn thing she wanted.

337

Clothes, cookbooks, goddamn wok. Then she started yelling for her share of the business. Gave her the business, all right. Cost me an axe and a cleaning bill, but it was fun. Wham, bam, thank you ma'am. Brains all over the carpet. Didn't know I could hit so hard. Life in the old gal yet. Eh, Appie?"

"While there's life, there's hope." Appie's voice sounded dazed. "Miffy, surely you can't mean — "

Miffy didn't sound as if she was paying any more attention to Appie then than she would have at any other time. "Make ol' Brad pay for the axe. His idea to fake the robbery. Wanted to plant the stuff on Sarah's Jew boy friend. Send him to the gas chamber. Where they all belong. Damn well better get my Bilbao looking glass back to me in one piece or I'll nail him to the wall. He knows I can do it. Didn't want to come in with me on the robberies at first. Too damn respectable. Huh! When was a Rovedock ever respectable? Send out a shipload of missionaries and rum. Good profit in opium. What the folks back home don't know won't hurt 'em. That's Brad. Half missionary, half — "

"Bradley Rovedock? Now, Miffy, surely you must realize this is the gin talking.

When I play back what you've just said — "

"Shove it, Appie. Go keep an eye on that niece of yours if you want something to do. Ol' Brad's out to get little Sarah. Can't leave the young girls alone, never could. That's how I nailed him. Alice found out. God knows how many. Welcome aboard, honeybunch. You can swim home later. Heave ho an' over we go. Gets bored after a while. So do I. Why I wanted to start the robberies in the first place. So damn dull here in the off season."

Wilson shut off the recorder. "I guess we don't have to listen to any more of that right now. You acted very wisely and sensibly, Mrs. Kelling."

"I did?"

Appie sounded astonished. "If only my husband could be alive to hear you say that! Sarah dear, about that flour on the kitchen floor — "

Sarah came out of her state of shock and leaned over to give her aunt a kiss. "Forget about the flour. Don't you realize you're a heroine?"

"Who, me? But I was only trying to do my smallest bestest. My one great regret is that I never got to play back that tape to Miffy. One could hardly do it that next morning before the funeral, and afterward it was too late."

"Save your regrets. If Miffy'd ever heard that recording when she was sober, it would have been too late for you."

"Surely you exaggerate, dear. Though after what she said about Alice B. — still, she'd hardly care to pay for having the carpet cleaned twice, would she?"

Appie watched anxiously as Chief Wilson sealed this invaluable piece of evidence in an envelope and stowed it with utmost care in his inside breast pocket.

"But aren't you going to give me back my tape now? How shall I ever get to sleep tonight without my traffic noises?"

Sarah had an inspiration. "Aunt Appie, I wonder whether what you'd like better than anything else would be to go straight back to Cambridge and spend the night in your own home?"

"Oh, Sarah, could I? You don't know how I've been yearning — though everyone has been so kind — and I did want to make myself useful."

"You've already done more than anyone could possibly have hoped. I'm sure Chief Wilson agrees."

"I certainly do, Mrs. Kelling. I'll write

you out a receipt for your tape right now. I'll need some depositions from you later and you'll probably have to testify at Rovedock's trial, but there's no reason why you have to hang around Ireson Town tonight. I'll have one of my men drive you. Or maybe Bittersohn would like to, now that you've got him off the hook."

"I can think of only one thing I'd enjoy more," said Max. "Come on, Aunt Appie, let's collect your luggage."

CHAPTER 23

"Say, Chief," said Jofferty, "if you don't need me any more, I'd better get these clams home to the Mrs. She must be fit to be tied by now."

"Phone her from here if you like, and explain what held you up," Sarah suggested.

"Thanks, I will. Give her a chance to simmer down by the time I get there."

Jofferty was heading for the telephone and Chief Wilson stowing away his notebook when Lionel charged into the main house waving a scrap of ragged metal.

"We've found a clue," he panted. "Don't glare at me like that, Sarah. My post is not deserted. Vare has come back to us. Without Tigger, I may add. She has decided alternative life-styles are not her cup of tea."

"I had a feeling she would," said Sarah,

recalling the terms of Miffy's will. "What did you find?"

"It was Woody who made the actual discovery. He sustained a minor laceration in the process, which I treated from my first-aid kit in accordance with standard emergency medical practice. He and Frank had been engaging in a spot of recreational by-play on the jetty."

"Yes, Lionel, they were horsing around," Sarah interpreted. "And Frank shoved Woody into the water and he cut himself on this thing. What is it?"

"The remains of a cylinder approximately four inches long, made of thin brass and precisely the inside diameter of a 12-gauge shotgun shell."

"So?"

"You are evidently not aware, Sarah, that the detonating device customarily employed in a signal cannon is a 12-gauge shotgun shell. A blank, naturally. However, there is no reason why some such object as this could not be inserted in the shell and fired from the cannon."

"Why should it have been?"

"One might expect you to be a little more, as my lads would express it, on the ball. To set fire to the boathouse, of course.

This metal is stained with chemicals. There is no doubt in my mind that it served as the casing for some sort of incendiary device. I have no equipment here to analyze the stains, but I daresay they will present no problem to a police chemist. In short, Sarah, while you were so unjustly heaping recriminations on us for setting fire to the boathouse, you were failing to realize that we had in fact been under bombardment. As you may recall, trial races were taking place that day. I participated myself, later on."

"I do remember," Sarah admitted. "Max and I heard a starting gun while we were having lunch. And Bradley Rovedock was firing it from *Perdita*, being too sportsman-like to compete in the races because everyone knew his boat was the fastest."

"It is true that Bradley was the starter," Lionel agreed. "The fact that he fired the cannon, however, does not negate my theory. The device could have been inserted in the barrel without his knowing."

"I'm sure it wasn't. You don't know this yet, but Bradley's just been arrested for murdering Miffy. Thanks to a brilliant piece of detection work by your mother."

"My mother?"

Lionel's eyes opened wide in amazement, then brightened in a glad surprise. Perhaps he was moved by filial devotion. Perhaps he, like Vare, was remembering that Appolonia Kelling Kelling was one of Miffy's heirs. Sarah thought she wouldn't remind him yet how vigorously the will was about to be contested by divers old pals whose homes Miffy had burgled to relieve the tedium of their absence. Why mar the verve with which Lionel rushed over to fling his arms around Appie?

"Mother, I'm so proud of you!"

"Oh, son!"

Appie wept blissfully in her boy's arms for a moment, then whipped out a tissue and wiped her impressive nose. "But tell me, dear, why did Bradley decide to burn down Sarah's boathouse?"

"Really, Mother, I couldn't say."

"I think I can," said Max Bittersohn. "One of the things I've managed to find out about Rovedock is that he's a director of the High Street Bank. The boathouse fire was another trial run, no doubt. I think he must have planned to burn down the house next. That would explain his playing around with the light switch the day we came, to suggest faulty wiring and take people's minds off incendiary devices. Then Sarah would have been in a real mess with the bank and he could either rush to the rescue or tighten the screws, as the case might be, until she fell swooning into his arms."

"I would not!" Sarah cried.

"Rovedock thought you would. I gather he's always had everything else he wanted. Why should he doubt that he could get you?"

"Especially since he appears to have pictured me as such a docile little thing," she had to agree. "That's why he wanted to poison me when he found out his plan wouldn't work."

"What do you mean, poison you?"

"Oh, didn't I tell you? He had the vial already in his hand when Sergeant Jofferty jumped him."

"My God!"

"Oh dear," said Appie. "I do feel so — Lionel dear, you won't mind too dreadfully if I go back to Cambridge tonight?"

"Not a bit, Mother, if that's what you want. As a matter of fact," Lionel's eyes gleamed even brighter, "I'll tell you what. We'll leave the boys here with Vare. That will further enrich her experience of motherhood and reinforce her decision to resume her accustomed role. Then I'll drive you back myself. You and I, Mummy, will spend a cozy night in our own two snug bedrooms, just like old times."

He even, of his own free will and without a whimper, carried his mother's luggage down to the van.

"Greater love hath no son," Sarah remarked after they'd gone. "Max, do you realize we two are all sole alone?"

"So we are. Well, well. What do you know about that?"

She moved closer to him. Her right hand stole up and loosened the top buttons of his shirt. "Want to pop some popcorn?" she mumured.

"Not now, you wanton hussy. Go slip into something uncomfortable."

"But why? Max darling, the war is over. We're at peace."

"That's what you think, baby. The final battle is yet to come. I'm taking you to meet my mother."

THORNDIKE PRESS HOPES you
have enjoyed this Large Print
book. All our Large Print titles
are designed for the easiest
reading, and all our books are
made to last. Other Thorndike
Press Large Print books are
available at your library,
through selected bookstores, or
directly from the publisher. For
more information about our
current and upcoming Large
Print titles, please send your
name and address to:

THORNDIKE PRESS
ONE MILE ROAD
P.O. Box 157
THORNDIKE, MAINE 04986

There is no obligation, of course.

LP
M   Cop. 1

MacLeod
    The Bilbao looking glass

SEP   1983